"I wanted to talk to you about Dilly Friedman," I said.

"Let's talk after I get through my run," Dicky said, no longer smiling, and I agreed.

I took a seat in the back and watched Fairfield go by. It really was an attractive place, full of nice, if uninventive, mostly pseudocolonial houses, green lawns, and bright flower beds. What I especially liked were the wide swaths of red and purple wildflowers that had been seeded in the open spaces. Pretty Fairfield—where a person had put a plastic bag over Dilly's head so that she would die. . . .

By Ellen Rawlings
Published by Fawcett Books:

THE MURDER LOVER
DEADLY HARVEST

DEADLY HARVEST

Ellen Rawlings

For Sandy
All the best.
Ellen Rawlings

FAWCETT GOLD MEDAL • NEW YORK

A Fawcett Gold Medal Book
Published by Ballantine Books
Copyright © 1997 by Ellen Rawlings
Excerpt from *The Murder Lover* copyright © 1997 by Ellen Rawlings.

http://www.randomhouse.com

Library of Congress Catalog Card Number: 97-90322

ISBN 0-449-14987-0

Manufactured in the United States of America

First Edition: September 1997

10 9 8 7 6 5 4 3 2 1

To my sister, Joan Cohen, my brother-in-law Gordon, and their children and grandchildren, with love

CHAPTER
1

How could I have known that an innocent association would end so violently? I was looking for a particular kind of person to write an article about, that's all. I was relieved when a neighbor of mine gave me Dilly Friedman's phone number; if this Dilly person worked out, I wouldn't have to start searching for a subject. "She's just what you need," the neighbor said. "Call her. I bet she'll say yes. She's very accommodating."

The first couple of times I phoned, I got her answering machine. It had one of those cutesy messages on it that are hard to listen to once, let alone three or four times. Nobody could say my machine was like that. My original message had disappeared somehow and been replaced with one provided by the manufacturer. It said "Leave a message" in a tinny voice that still managed to sound commanding. I always meant to replace it, but I never did.

When I finally got through to Dilly, I explained that I was a freelance writer and wanted to do an article on her and the inner-city school where she taught. Dilly said sure; she'd love to talk about her school. That wasn't exactly what I had in mind, but I decided to wait until I met her to go into specifics. The next day was a Saturday, and she didn't have to work, so we agreed to meet then. Since I was self-employed, I made my own hours. I would see her at one o'clock at the Scandia restaurant.

"I'm a blonde with blue eyes," she said. "I'll be wearing a red blouse and red skirt. I love red. Don't you?"

"Sure," I said, although I don't think I owned anything red. I went on to describe myself so that at least one of us would recognize the other.

I got to the restaurant a little before one. I spotted her as soon as she walked in. Her light hair was down to her shoulders and spilled in frothy bangs over her forehead to just above her eyes. She was of medium height. She wasn't bad looking but fell short of being really attractive because her nose was kind of sharp and her mouth, bright red and thick with lipstick, was too wide. I put her age at the middle twenties.

"You're Rachel Crowne, right?" she said with an effervescent smile. "Your description was good, except that you didn't say you were pretty."

I felt I could work well with this woman.

We each ordered a turkey sandwich and coffee and carried our trays to a table. Dilly got a few looks as we went. It was probably because of her clothes. They were red, from her neck to her feet. Even her stockings were red. To say her outfit was colorful would be like saying Mozart was a pretty good composer.

"Do you dress like that when you teach?" I asked, hoping my question sounded like idle curiosity and not censure. Again, the smile. "Are you kidding? My principal would kill me. It's fun to loosen up on the weekends, though; don't you think?"

I looked down at my gray sweats and blue canvas Keds. If she thought I was being weekend casual, she was wrong. I wore clothes like that every day. Fortunately, in Fairfield, the way a person dressed wasn't important. People looking no more formal than I did at that moment showed up in all but our fanciest restaurant.

Dilly patted my hand. "Tell me about your project."

I told her that I wanted to write an article on how she'd overcome the culture shock she must have experienced teaching at an inner-city school.

She looked surprised. "What culture shock?"

"My neighbor says you work at Nettie Blue," I said, referring to an elementary school in one of the worst slums in Baltimore. I figured just saying its name would explain what I meant.

She pushed the bangs out of her eyes, then nodded.

"Well, obviously, you and your pupils don't come from the same backgrounds. For one thing, you're white, and from what I've been told, the student body is almost one hundred percent black."

"I guess so," she said.

I assumed the uncertainty was over my numbers, not her race.

"What I'm interested in writing about is the culture clash between you and your kids and how you got around it, if you did."

"I don't know what you mean."

I wondered if she was dumb. "You must be kidding. You come from a middle-class background, right?" She nodded, making her bangs flap against her forehead. "The kids at Nettie Blue don't," I said.

"I guess not. I don't usually notice stuff like that."

She touched her lower lip with her index finger, then put her hand down. There was a smear of lipstick on the finger. "I must have forgotten to blot my lips," she said apologetically. I noticed that her eye teeth were crooked; I found that kind of appealing.

In fact, I found her appealing. It wasn't just her obvious

sweetness and easygoing attitude. I sensed the insecurity of a little girl abandoned underneath everything else. It touched the maternal aspects of my personality.

She wiped the red off her fingertip onto her napkin. "Tell me something about you," she said.

I wasn't used to being in that role; I felt a little uncomfortable. "There's not much to tell. I've been doing this kind of work for several years. I like it, and it's going pretty well. I've been married twice. Now I'm single. I don't have children."

"I've never been married," she said. She looked wistful. "I have children, though."

"Oh yeah?"

"Sure. My kids at school. I'm a special education teacher. I get some of the most screwed-up kids in that neighborhood."

"That's what I mean," I said. "I've heard about the problems these kids can have. How could you, coming from such a vastly different background, be prepared for stuff like this? How do you deal with it? Are you shocked, or are you blasé by now? And why do you keep working at that school? Those are some of the things I hope you'll talk about."

Dilly sat back against her chair. She shook her head. "I think you have the wrong person, Rachel. I can't answer your questions."

"Why not?"

"It's like this: I'd guess if you were around these kids, you'd see problems, maybe unsolvable ones. That's not what I see. I see Cleome, who's smart but can't do math very well because of a learning disability. I see Ahmed, who's great in math but reads on a first-grade level, and Lee, who always says the wrong thing and gets himself beaten up. Some of them are lovable, some are a little harder to love, but all of them are challenging and fascinating. That's what I see. I wouldn't want to work with kids from the suburbs. It's not that I wouldn't care about them. It's that they wouldn't need me as much as Cleome and the others. I help out my kids, and they appreciate me for it."

I saw something, too. I saw behind the chirpy exterior, behind even the unsure little girl, somebody who was lonely and with an urgent hunger to be needed.

I was touched by what I saw. Maybe that's why I decided to jettison my culture clash idea and do an article on what interested her. Just as I started to tell her so, she began getting up from her seat. I clamped my hand on her arm. Whoever said I have tunnel vision—and the number is legion—would have known I wasn't about to let go of this opportunity.

"Let me write about you and your pupils," I said, pulling her down. "It will be a great story, Dilly. You'll want it to be told."

She was firmly back in her chair, so I took my hand off her. I waited.

"I don't know," she said, pushing at the bangs. Why did some people go around insisting on looking like a sheepdog? "There could be problems. My principal might not like my talking about how shitty the school is. We don't have enough books for everybody, and my classroom is in the basement. Literally. We can't even see outside. Also, some of the parents might not like it."

"We don't have to say what school it is," I said. "We can give it a fictitious name. We won't mention the neighborhood, either. Nettie Blue isn't the only school in Baltimore next to a housing project, is it?"

"No."

"Well, then, no problem."

"I *would* like to let people be made aware of what

these kids go through," she said. "Then maybe everyone would stop blaming them and wanting to take their free lunches away."

Dilly looked as though she might cry. I thought about buying her a pastry to cheer her up, but it seemed inappropriate while we were talking about children deprived of lunch. "Let me get you some more coffee," I said, and rushed up to the counter to order it. When I came back, she appeared less upset.

"Do you really think this article might help?" she said.

"Maybe."

"Then let's do it."

"Great. Do you want to start now?"

She sighed. "If you don't mind, I'd rather not. I don't like getting worked up. I want to be calmer first."

"Good idea," I said, although I felt disappointed. "How about tonight?"

"Tonight?" She put a hand through the blond bangs. "I can't. I'm expecting company. How about tomorrow?"

"I can't do it tomorrow, or the next day, either," I said. "I've got three other things to finish. How about Tuesday after work?"

We agreed to meet at her house then. She gave me her address, and I gave me my card in case she had to get in touch with me.

"I'll be wanting to visit your school, too," I said. "I'll need to interview some of the students."

She giggled. "I hope you have bulletproof glass in your car. There are a lot of guns around there, and sometimes they go off."

"Are you serious?"

"I am. But don't worry. Call me before you come, and I'll have someone outside watching for you."

"Is that what you do, have someone watching out for you every day?"

"Not me. Nobody ever tries to hurt me, not recently, anyway."

"What do you mean? Have there been incidents?"

She stood. "I don't mean anything. I'll see you Tuesday."

I didn't try to detain her. "Sure," I said. I never saw Dilly Friedman again.

CHAPTER
2

I got a phone call Tuesday morning, at 7:00 A.M., maybe a little earlier. It woke me up. Without identifying himself, the caller said, "Are you Rachel Crowne?" The voice was flat, emotionless. It didn't sound like anyone I knew.

I said, "Yes."

"My sister was murdered Saturday night."

I still didn't know who the speaker was. "What's your name?" I said.

"I'm sorry." The tone stayed flat. "I'm Benny Friedman. I'm talking about Dilly Friedman. You were a friend of hers, right? I found your card in her house."

He sounded like someone who'd taken several Valium. I could have used one myself. Dilly Friedman. I couldn't believe it.

"I was wondering if you knew about it," the emotionless voice went on without waiting for a response.

"No, I didn't. Did it happen at her school?"

"Her school? Why would you think that?"

"She said something about it being a rough environment."

"She was murdered in her house. That's where I found your card."

Apparently, he considered it important that she had it, although I handed them out pretty freely and had a stack

8

of other people's cards stuffed into my wallet. "I gave it to her," I said. "I was going to write an article on her and figured she might want it."

"Yes."

"Do the police know who did it? Has the person been caught?"

Maybe he didn't hear me, because he said, "She told me about the article. I live in Philadelphia. That's long-distance. Usually we speak to each other every other Saturday; we take turns paying. It wasn't our weekend to talk, but she called me specially Saturday afternoon to tell me about the article. She was excited about it."

She must have made the call after her meeting with me at the Mall that day. Maybe I was the last person other than the murderer to see her alive. I didn't think it necessary to share this possibility with Benny, although I knew I would have to inform the police. "I hadn't started it yet," I said. "I just discussed the idea with her and took some preliminary notes. Look, never mind that. Tell me how she was killed."

"I want to tell you, but not over the phone. Will you come here? I'm at Dilly's house."

I hesitated because I had been planning to go to the Athletic Club a little later in the morning to work out. Exercise is a necessity for me; I need it like I need eating and reading.

"Please come," Benny Friedman said. "I don't want to be alone here anymore."

I couldn't turn him down. "I'll be there in a half an hour," I said.

Dilly lived about two miles from me. I could have driven to her house in five minutes. I intended to go on foot, though. Getting there and back would be my exercise.

Does that make me sound practical? I'm not, usually. But, as I said, exercise is important to me.

"I'd better warn you," I told him. "I'll be walking. I'll be sweaty when I get to Dilly's place. I want you to know that I mean no disrespect."

It took several minutes for me to convince him that I didn't want him to pick me up in his car. Finally, he gave in.

Except for the news about Dilly, it was a nice day. The middle of April meant the buds and new leaves were out. The air smelled clean and invigorating, no easy trick in a city situated on both sides of a major corridor running between Baltimore and Washington.

The name of my city is Fairfield. It's made up of eight self-contained villages, which means each one includes a supermarket, dry cleaner, Chinese restaurant, and liquor store. Some of the villages even have bookstores. It's a nice place, definitely not where a person expects a murder to happen.

I walked past narrow town houses, like mine, with small plots of ground and detached houses with much larger ones. I walked past one cul-de-sac after another, along bike paths surrounded by green open spaces. I reached Dilly's village, which was called Harvey Drew, after some obscure former landowner. A half hour of walking had just about done it.

Benny must have been watching for me. The door opened before I could ring the bell. "Are you Rachel Crowne?"

I nodded, then wiped sweat off my forehead.

"Come in, please."

I looked down. Instead of steps there was a wooden ramp—the sort of thing needed for a wheelchair-bound person or someone permanently on crutches. Dilly hadn't had anything wrong with her legs that I'd noticed. I wondered why it had been put there.

Benny Friedman was tall and thin, with bright gold hair and blue eyes, like Dilly. I guessed his age to be about the same as mine. He was wearing a black suit with a white shirt and black tie. He looked tired and funereal.

He gestured with his hand toward the living room. I followed him.

Dilly's house reminded me a lot of her. The sofa was covered in exuberant red-blue-and-green stripes. The curtains at the windows were red with blue polka dots. The red rug almost matched the red in the sofa, but didn't quite make it. There were plants everywhere, some in green pots, some in red.

I seated myself. Then, for the second time, I asked, "How did she die?"

Benny took a chair across from me. "Somebody hit her on the head and then suffocated her."

He'd probably had to identify her remains. I pictured the scene at the Baltimore morgue. I made myself put it out of my mind.

"The police haven't found the murderer," he said.

"What can I do?"

"I don't know anybody here. I told you; I'm from Philadelphia. I'm the only family Dilly has. Had."

"I'm sorry," I said, not knowing what else to say. Empty platitudes aren't my style.

"I want you to write about her."

I shook my head. I didn't have enough for a piece. I had expected to watch her interacting with the kids at school and then ask her questions. Now that wouldn't happen.

If Benny saw my gesture, he ignored it. "She was thrilled that you were going to feature her in an article. I told you that already, right? Her fifteen minutes of fame, she said."

She was going to have them anyway, I thought. Her murder was sure to be written up in the papers. I kept the thought to myself.

"I've got to tell you something," I said. "I hardly knew her. Someone gave me her name, and I only spoke to her once in person."

"Then you weren't a friend?"

"No, though I might have become one. I liked her."

"She liked you, too. I could tell. So, will you do it? It would be a memorial to her, and those kids. She really cared about them. She used to tell me about them all the time."

"I don't know, Benny. I'll have to think about it."

He gave me a pleading look. "Maybe you could also find out why someone wanted her dead."

"Me? I'm not a cop."

"No, but I'll bet you get around. You ask questions. People talk to you. And you seem shrewd." I must have given him a look that said I didn't know how to take his last remark, because he said, "I mean that as a compliment. I'd guess not too many people fool you." He stopped, sucked in a breath, then said, "How old are you, if you don't mind my asking?"

"I'm thirty-five." And looking good, I could have added. At least that's what people told me.

"Dilly was twenty-six. You've lived nine more years already than she did."

Too bad this guy was a male. He would have made a perfect Jewish mother, at least in the guilt-inducing department.

I could see by the way he talked to me that the tranquilizer was beginning to wear off. A feistier personality was taking over. So was the pain of his loss.

"I'm sorry," I said, "but this just isn't my kind of thing. I figure it was a robbery that went bad. Wasn't it?"

He laughed without humor. "Look around. Is this a place someone would want to rob?"

It wasn't. Except for the TV set, a VCR, and a portable phone, I couldn't see anything, at least in the living room, that a burglar would covet. The furniture was cheap. I knew that because when I put my hand on the back of the sofa, I felt staples. The two armchairs looked as though they were held together with spit. The bookcase was one of those fifty-nine-dollar folding things.

Okay, it wasn't a robbery. I didn't want to ask, but I had to. "Was she molested?"

"You mean raped?" His voice cracked. "No."

He sat back, then started to mutter. I couldn't hear the words, but I picked up the hysteria in his tone.

"What is it?"

"You asked if she was raped. The answer is, no, she was roped. That's how she was strangled, with a plastic bag and a piece of rope."

Talk about overkill; somebody was really determined to see her dead. I said, "If she wasn't killed because of robbery, and she wasn't killed for sexual reasons, why was she killed?"

He stared at me. "I don't know."

I remembered her saying that a person, or people, had tried to harm her in the past. "Did she mention that anyone was angry with her?" I asked.

He shook his head. "Of course not. No one ever gets angry with Dilly. She's too sweet and good-natured."

"What about failed relationships?" I said, thinking about my own and the bitterness they'd engendered on both sides. "I know she'd never been married because she'd told me so, but was she ever engaged?"

He got up, paced a little, and then came to a stop behind one of the chairs. "Never married, never engaged," he said, "and that was a surprise to me and everyone else who knew her. We all figured she'd marry young. She would have made a perfect wife and mother."

I wondered what his idea of perfection was. Maybe if I'd known more about perfection, my two husbands wouldn't have divorced me. Maybe not. It wasn't my fault that I couldn't conceive the child my first husband wanted. I still thought he was a bastard for having walked out on me. I wanted a child, too, desperately, but I wouldn't have left him if the problem had been his. As for husband number two, some of that fiasco was my responsibility. Since I couldn't have a baby, I married one. Then I refused to baby him, so he walked, too.

It was pointless to think about past mistakes. I made myself stop. I said, "Did she have a boyfriend?"

"You know, you're asking me the same things the cops did."

"Would you rather I didn't?"

"No, I don't mind. What's the difference? She had a boyfriend for a while, Murray Rothman, I think his name was. He lives in Fairfield, too. Nothing came of it, though."

"What about friends?"

He looked confused.

"What's the matter?"

"I'm sure she had friends. At the least, you'd think she'd be friendly with the people she worked with. But when I went to call, to let them know what had happened to her, the only names in her address book were doctors and a dentist and the woman she rents this house from. There weren't any friends, not even you. How could that be?"

I couldn't imagine. First of all, I would have bet even Genghis Khan and Hitler had friends. Secondly, she was lovable. "That's strange," I said.

"It's all strange. And crazy. I had to identify her, you

know. I had to look at her face. It was . . ." He bent his head and cried.

It always seems worse to me when a man cries than when a woman does. Maybe that's because I've seen so few adult men do it. Their tears seem to be wrenched from within, as though the crying is as painful to them as its cause. Benny Friedman sounded like he'd lost his whole world. I murmured some stuff. He cried. I said I wouldn't leave yet. He kept crying. After a while, I said I guessed I'd write the article.

CHAPTER
3

Some people think that writers are a different breed from other folks. I wouldn't know because I'm not acquainted with that many of us. Actually, I'm not acquainted with a lot of people here in Fairfield. I need to spend time alone, doing research and writing. Besides, I enjoy being by myself. My head—imagination, ability to fantasize, whatever you want to call it—is always going. I like to be tuned in to it and listen. A self-entertainer, that's me.

What I do besides write is work out, a lot, and ride my bike. I'm also good friends with Nancy Martin, the rich, coolly gorgeous, and elegant owner of the *Howard County Target*, a local bimonthly magazine that sometimes publishes my articles, and Tom Brant, the cop who lives next door to me. Other than those two, I guess I don't have close friends.

As for a love life, at the time Dilly was killed I didn't have much of one of those, either. My boyfriend was Jordan Goldman, a divorced guy with two children. Perhaps I should call him a divorced guy–widower. His ex-wife was murdered shortly before I met him. I helped solve the case.

Jordan spent most of his time after the murder with his kids. I thought that was admirable, but it was hard on me. When Dilly Friedman was killed, Jordan was in Florida with them. He was going to be away for two weeks. I hadn't been invited to join them.

It was during that period that I attended Dilly's memorial service, which a few of her neighbors had arranged. Benny Friedman had returned to Philadelphia after having his sister's remains cremated. Cremation used to be strictly against Jewish law and still is to Orthodox and Conservative Jews, but I guess her brother wasn't aware of that or maybe he didn't care.

I called Nancy to ask if she wanted to go to the service with me. "Did I know her?" she said.

"No."

"Then why should I go?"

"To keep me company."

"Not good enough."

"She was murdered."

"Okay, I'll go."

The service was held at the Interfaith Center, which was in the same village where Dilly had lived. It was a one-story brown brick building designed for all the activities of the Christian and Jewish groups in Fairfield. The idea for the center was to save the various religions from having to spend money building expensive houses of worship and to foster a spirit of ecumenicism. Amazingly, for the most part the idea worked. As I said before, this was a nice place—if you didn't count Dilly's murder.

The service was set for 10:00 A.M. The auditorium was filled with at least twenty-four rows of metal chairs, twelve on each side of the center aisle. At the front of the room was the ark. Inside it was the scroll containing the hand-written Torah, the five books of Moses. The doors of the ark were covered by rich blue velvet hangings with crowned lions embroidered in gold thread. Someone had placed a lectern several feet in front of the doors.

The room was jammed. There were people there of both sexes and all ages and colors. Benny must be crazy, I thought, or Dilly had had more than one phone book.

The service had already begun when Nancy and I arrived. We stood near the front of the room until two men got up and gave us their places. I'm all for women's lib, but there's no use being a fanatic when a good seat comes along.

The woman speaking was in a wheelchair. She looked to be in her early fifties. She had a delicate face, with a narrow jaw that barely seemed to provide enough room for a full complement of teeth. Her short hair was curly and blond, with only a few strands of gray at the front and sides. Her eyes were light brown, ringed by shadows. Pain lines were etched around her mouth. Despite the warm weather, she wore a high-necked black dress, trimmed with lace, and had a blanket covering her lap and extending to the tops of her dainty black shoes.

"Dilly was very dear to me," she said in a gentle, wavering voice. "I knew her for years. I rented her the house she lived in."

Aha, I thought. That's why there was a ramp instead of steps.

I missed the first few words of what she said next. ". . . engaged to my son before he died; she would have been my daughter had he lived. She was part of my life, a very important part. Now she is gone." A single tear trickled down her face, more touching to me than an uninhibited torrent. I felt like crying myself.

I turned my head to look at Nancy. As usual, she appeared detached. She was so . . . Olympian.

Never mind her. Benny Friedman hadn't told me that Dilly had been engaged. In fact, he had given me the definite impression that she'd never gotten that far in a relationship with a man. I wondered what I'd missed in those first few words. Had the woman said that Dilly was engaged to her son, or about to be? Even if the latter were the case, it seemed odd to me that Benny hadn't known about the guy. I'll have to check on that, I thought, and then felt myself grimace. I'd promised to write about Dilly and her students, not try to find out why someone murdered her. I hoped I'd remember that.

The delicate-looking lady went on for a while longer, offering up aspects of Dilly's life that showed the younger woman to be a loving, good-humored person. Finally, she stopped. Another woman came forward, kissed the speaker, then rolled her chair to one side of the room. There was silence, followed by foot-shuffling and throat-clearing, but no one else came up.

A slight sound behind me, like a seat being shoved out of the way, made me turn my head. Four guys were sitting next to one another. They all looked to be around Dilly's age. One of them stood.

He was about five nine, thin, with light hair and eyes, and an intense manner that I had a feeling was habitual with him. He was dressed in a black suit, a white shirt, and an innocuous gray tie. He introduced himself as the Reverend Robert McCauley. He said he was a friend of Dilly's from college days and wanted to recite part of a poem that expressed her nature better than he ever could. He cleared his throat, before saying with feeling,

She was a queen of noble Nature's crowning,
A smile of hers was like an act of grace;
She had no winsome looks, no pretty frowning,
Like daily beauties of the vulgar race:
But if she smiled, a light was on her face.

At that point, he broke down and had to ease himself back in his seat. The three guys with him seemed embarrassed by McCauley's display of emotion. Maybe they didn't care for his spouting poetry, either.

I heard a high-pitched feminine wail near the front of the room, but I couldn't tell who it came from. One thing I did know—Benny had had it all wrong. The affection for his sister was almost palpable.

So why had Dilly been killed?

The Reverend McCauley was replaced by one of the three rabbis who had posts in Fairfield. I'd never spoken with him, but I knew his name. He was Rabbi Neufeld, about thirty and very cute. "I may convert," said Nancy, who was High Church Episcopalian. I nudged her with my elbow to be quiet.

"Dilly didn't belong to my congregation," the rabbi said in an accent that marked him as a southerner. "Although Jewish, she didn't belong to any of the congregations. But she exemplified everything Judaism stands for. She was unfailingly kind and charitable. She gave of herself, both in time and in money, to anyone who asked her, and many did.

"I want to tell you about the first time I met her, at one of the nursing homes where she volunteered. I asked her what Dilly stood for. She told me that her given name was Delilah. 'My mother wanted to give me a Jewish name,' she said, 'so she took one from the Bible.' When I pointed out that Delilah had been a Philistine, she said she knew that, but she never told her mother because she didn't want to make her feel bad. That was our Delilah, not a murderous Philistine but a good young woman through and through. She will be greatly missed."

By now I could hear people crying around me. One or two who got up to speak had to sit down because they were sobbing too hard to talk. I didn't feel great myself.

After the service, I mingled with the crowd, and Nancy went off to talk to Rabbi Neufeld. The woman in the wheelchair introduced herself to me as Etta Pearl. Though she was obviously in distress, there was something light and charming about her.

I introduced myself. "Were you a good friend of Dilly?" she said. "I talked to her rather frequently but don't remember your name ever coming up."

"I barely knew her," I said, "and not for very long."

She smiled and touched my hand. "It was certainly generous of you to come, then. I think most of the people here knew her for quite a while."

"I believe I would have liked to."

She studied me for a moment. "How did you meet her?"

I explained about my project. She seemed interested. "Would you like me to try to find another teacher for you? I know some. That's because I volunteer at our elementary school frequently."

"It's nice of you to do that."

She sat up straighter and gave me a winsome look. "Not really. I want children to understand that even handicapped individuals, even those in wheelchairs like me, have something to contribute. So many people take it for granted that being crippled means you can't be productive. I want to show them that's wrong."

She paused, then said, "Besides, I have to fill my life with something. Now that Everett's dead . . ." Her voice trailed off.

"Everett?"

Her face flushed. "My son. My only child. He's dead. I . . . I've tried, but I haven't gotten over it."

"When my mom died, my grandmother said you can recover from the death of a husband, but you never get over the death of a child."

The flush receded. "She was right. How old were you when your mother died?"

"Nine."

"I'm sorry."

Here was this woman caught up in her own grief, over Dilly as well as her son, and yet she had troubled to commiserate with me. I admired her for that. I wondered how her son had died and what caused her to become crippled, but, of course, I couldn't ask.

I said, "Getting back to what we were talking about, I'm going to turn down your offer of finding me someone else to interview. I have some information on Dilly, and I mean to pay a visit to her students. That should do it. If you have anything especially enlightening about her to tell me, though, I'd appreciate it if you'd get in touch."

She looked as though she was considering something. I waited. "Do you know about the group of friends Dilly went around with in college?" she asked.

I shook my head.

"It consisted of Dilly and five fellows, including my son. They met at the University of Maryland; that's where they went to school. According to Everett, they were inseparable." She hesitated. "Do you think it's odd that a girl would pal around with five boys?"

"You're asking the wrong person," I said. "I stayed as close to my four brothers as they'd let me. I liked hanging out with boys."

"Then I guess it must be all right," she said, and touched my hand again.

"Who were the male members of the group?" I asked.

She seemed taken aback. "Why?"

"I don't know. I might want to get in touch with them."

"Really? Very well. You were sitting in front of them. One was Bob McCauley. He recited that poem." She laughed. "He always liked to do that sort of thing. Another was Jim Cohen. He's here somewhere. I saw him earlier. He's young and blond, and he has presence. You'll know him when you see him."

I stuck my hand in my purse and fished around for paper and pen. I needed to write down the names; I'd never remember all of them. I found a pen but no paper and gave up.

Mrs. Pearl said, "The fourth, the shaggy-looking fellow with the beard, is . . . Oh dear, I can't remember his name. I can't remember the fifth one's name, either." She gave me a loopy smile. "I must be getting senile."

I smiled back. "I'm sure you're not." I uttered a few more polite words, then started to back off. I wanted to find the guys she'd talked about.

I didn't see any of them, but I did meet one of Dilly's neighbors. She was a woman of about thirty named Joan. She had short, curly brown hair, like mine. In fact, she looked a little like me. I introduced myself and told her I was planning to write about Dilly. "She was lovely," she said. "A real friend." She seemed to think about that, then said, "Well, not exactly a friend. She never called me or dropped by to visit, but when I got in touch with her she was always willing to do me a favor. You know, she'd feed my cat when I went away, and water the plants. She did a good job, too. She was conscientious."

"That's nice," I said. "Why do you think she never called and visited?"

Joan sighed. "I don't know. She never went out to lunch with me, or went shopping, or to a movie. She wasn't a girlfriend. She'd give you the shirt off her back if you asked for it, but she wouldn't get chummy with you. She wouldn't let you get close to her." She sighed again. "Too bad. I always had the feeling she'd make a great pal."

Maybe Benny wasn't wrong after all.

I spoke with several other people after that, including

colleagues of hers from the school where she taught. If I kept up the conversation and asked questions, sooner or later every one of them said about the same thing Joan had: Dilly was friendly and giving, but she wouldn't let you get too near to her.

I spotted a tall, blond man in the crowd. I couldn't have said whether or not he had presence, but someone called him Jim. That was enough to make me stick around.

This Jim was a young, good-looking guy, wearing a well-cut dark suit and highly polished shoes. He was covering territory. I watched him for a while. He made me think of someone who was running for office.

When he worked his way over to me, he stuck out his hand and pumped mine. His was warm and firm. "I'm James Cohen," he said. "I know I've never met you before because if I had I'd remember you. Your eyes are a beautiful shade of blue."

Was he coming on to me at a memorial service? I started to suggest that his behavior was not appropriate, only not couched so politely, but his expression made me doubt myself. He seemed sincere.

Had I heard his name before Mrs. Pearl gave it to me? I felt sure I'd come across it somewhere. Then I remembered. He *was* running for office, for the county council. "Were you a neighbor of Dilly's?" he said.

"No, not really. In fact, I live in Brent Dane Village. I met Dilly through a neighbor of hers. I was going to write an article about her and the school where she taught."

"Is that so? You're a writer, then." He looked at me appraisingly. "I'm running for a position on the county council," he said. "Maybe since you've lost your subject you might be interested in getting another." He laughed. "I mean, you could write about me."

God, this service was for Dilly, and the guy was trying to promote himself. It would be a cold day in Hell, I thought, before I'd do anything for him.

My face must have told him what I thought about his suggestion. "I'm really upset about Dilly," he said, touching my shoulder. "We were close."

I didn't believe him, and not just because nobody else had claimed that distinction. "How close?"

He shrugged and laughed. "Actually, not very in the last few years. We went through college together. We were in the same class and graduated together. People used to call us the Six-Pack, because there were six of us, and you could find us together. Not to mention that we all liked beer."

"Six, huh? You, Dilly, and who else?"

"There was Everett Pearl. . . ."

"Mrs. Pearl's son."

He looked uncomfortable. "Yes. He's dead."

"She told me. She also said the rest of your group was here, but I don't see them."

"They left right after the service," he said.

"Could you give me their names and numbers? Mrs. Pearl told me some of their names, but I'd like to know all of them."

He seemed to freeze. "Why?"

Before I could repeat what I'd told Etta Pearl, he said, "Got to say hello to the rabbis. They're important people in the community." James Cohen walked off.

I started to follow him but decided to let him go. It wouldn't be hard to get his phone number, and I could contact him another day.

After that, I talked to the principal at Dilly's school. I asked for and got her permission to interview some of the staff and pupils there about Dilly. Then I talked to a few of the teachers she'd worked with. It was the same story.

Dilly was sweet, she was generous, she'd do anything for you, but she'd never go anywhere with you after school. Friendship, as much as there was, was confined to the time between the opening and closing bells.

It was odd. I wondered what had been going on with her. But, surely, whatever it was, it wasn't a reason to murder her. Or was it?

CHAPTER
4

Tom Brant, the guy who lived in the town house next to mine, was a Howard County homicide detective. As I mentioned before, he was also one of my best friends. After I got back from Dilly's memorial service and changed into my usual scruffy clothes, I went to visit him. I figured he'd know something about the murder even if he hadn't been assigned to the case. The squad wasn't that large, and the detectives talked among themselves.

As to whether he'd tell me anything that couldn't be found in the newspapers, I thought he would. That was because he lived alone. He didn't have anyone else around to discuss things with after he got home.

The other reason was that he trusted me because I knew his worst secret. He did needlepoint in his spare time. Not those things out of kits, either. Tom designed and did the most beautiful wall hangings I'd ever seen. They were free-form shapes, with stones, pieces of gold- or silver-colored leather, and other unusual objects embedded in them. He let people think his aunt had done them, even put her initials on them. I had found him out by barging into his house one day and catching him at it. After I agreed never to tell another living soul, and he agreed to spare my life conditional upon my keeping my word, we became real buddies.

And buddies we stayed. We never let sex complicate our relationship. Even when he was feeling horny, or I was, we knew not to get entangled like that. The friendship was more important to us, so we were careful about it.

I rang the bell, and he let me in. His thick, dark hair was rumpled and he was shoeless, so I figured he'd been sleeping.

He scowled at me. "What do you want?"

"Such charm," I said, and pushed past him, taking in the smell of stale beer as I entered his living room.

His blinds were down, so the room was pretty dark. I didn't have trouble finding my way around the furniture, though, because I knew what the room looked like and where things were: a green sofa in front of the long wall and matching armchairs facing it. One bookcase on the short, windowless wall containing mostly texts about how to do criminal investigations, along with a smattering of psychology and sociology books. A couple of tables that didn't match. There was nothing to make *Architectural Digest* want to feature his place in their next issue.

Actually, his house looked better than mine, which was an example of early graduate student that I'd never gotten around to fixing up. Except for some handsome, nicely framed contemporary prints and a few pieces of mostly reproduction sculpture, my town house was shabby and undistinguished; it could have belonged to anybody who didn't care very much about what she lived in. Caring was something I planned to do later in my life, after my career was more solid.

I went to his windows and opened the blinds, ignoring his annoyed look; I wanted to be able to see his expression when I asked him questions. Then I sat down.

Tom stared at me.

"What is it?"

"Don't you have any better clothes than that?"

I had changed into a faded blue denim shorts outfit and thought I looked rather nice. I wasn't hurt by his remark, but I wasn't thrilled, either. "Don't you?" I said.

"What's the matter with what I'm wearing?"

Since he had on equally faded jeans and a shapeless white T-shirt, I didn't see how he could even ask. I looked at his bare feet. I said, "Ugh. Put your shoes on."

"What's wrong with my feet?"

"I don't like hairy toes."

"So, go home."

"Nope," I said. "I want to talk to you about something. I recently found out about the Dilly Friedman murder."

"Yeah? How'd you do that?"

"Her brother called and told me."

He frowned. "Why'd he call you? Is he a friend of yours?"

I decided not to tell him right away that I'd been with Dilly that past Saturday. If I did, he'd start asking all the questions. I shook my head. "I was sort of acquainted with her, and he found my card at her house. Also, I went to her memorial service today. People were talking about the murder. Never mind all that. What do you know that didn't make the six o'clock news?"

"Nothing. I don't know anything. Go away."

I settled myself as comfortably as I could into the sofa. I was small, and it was big, to fit Tom. He was over six feet, with the beginnings of an above-the-belt pot that guys get and a heavy beard that caused him to have to shave twice a day. He obviously had lots of active male hormones.

"Whose case is it?" I asked.

"Not mine. That's why I don't know anything."

"Sure you do," I said. "So what can you tell me?"

"You're a pest."

"What else?"

He glared at me. "You know what you are? What's that Yiddish word that means a person who can't mind her own business?"

"A yenta."

"That's it."

"Tell me," I said.

Tom sighed and sat down across from me. The chair creaked. "Somebody hit her with a heavy object, then put a plastic bag over her head and asphyxiated her. There, are you satisfied?"

"Did the police find the heavy object?"

"If we did, do you think I'd call it that? We haven't found anything. Nobody can think of a motive. And nobody saw anything. We've been asking around."

"Dilly was a nice woman," I said.

"Yeah? I thought you didn't know her very well."

That's when I told him about my meeting with her that past Saturday.

"You'll have to talk to the police about it," he said. I nodded.

He combed his hair with his fingers. "She sounds nice. It's too bad about her."

I knew he meant it. His toughness wasn't an act. It wasn't just skin-deep, either. Nothing lousy the human race did surprised him. Still, he had feelings for decent people like Dilly.

"Why do you think she was killed?" I said. "Take a guess."

"I can't. Why do you?"

"Her brother said it wasn't robbery or rape."

"Doesn't seem to have been."

His communication skills were starting to annoy me. "Talk," I said.

He shrugged. "Okay, let's consider robbery. Whoever came in didn't break in, so she must have known the guy."

"Besides," I said, "she didn't appear to have anything worth stealing."

"Right. So it had to be something else. So far, though, we don't have anything else. She was never married. She didn't even have a boyfriend who could have offed her."

"She used to, a guy named Murray Rothman. Her brother told me."

"He told us, too. We already spoke to Rothman. He's got a perfect alibi. He was in the hospital the day she was killed, recuperating from a hernia operation."

"Her brother said she didn't seem to have real friends."

"Yeah. That's weird, isn't it? Even a mean broad like you has a friend or two."

"But if one of them is you . . ." I said.

He grinned. "Okay. I'll stop picking on you. Tell me what you think about the no-friends thing."

"I agree it's odd, especially because of the way she was. I only met her once, but she made a really good impression on me. She was sweet, Tom. A little ditsy, too, but I wouldn't think that would scare anyone off. She was the kind of person who should have had lots of friends. In fact, she used to, when she was in college. She hung around with a group called the Six-Pack. It was Dilly and five guys. One of them is dead. The other four were at the memorial service."

"Is that how you found out about them?"

I nodded.

"Who are they?"

I told him the two names I knew, Cohen's and the Reverend McCauley's. "You can ask Jim Cohen for the others," I said.

He yawned. "I doubt that we will. If they are people who only used to be her friends, it's not likely they'd have anything to do with her murder."

I couldn't disagree.

"So why did she stop having friends?" Tom asked.

"According to the people I spoke with at her memorial service, it was because she didn't want them. She was generous and kind, but she didn't care to socialize. From what I heard today, she was beating people off right and left."

He gave me a cynical look. "Maybe that's not true. You know how everyone is about speaking ill of the dead."

"Yes. Maybe. I don't think so, though. The affection seemed genuine."

He let that pass.

"Any suspects?" I asked. "You said it probably was someone she knew. Or maybe it was someone she didn't know but expected, like a repairman."

"Maybe. If that's true, there's no record of one that we can find. As for its being some mutt off the street who does this to get his jollies, I don't think so."

I sat back, genuinely interested in hearing what he had to say. After all, he was an experienced detective while I was . . . I didn't know what I was, why I liked this kind of thing so much. I just knew I did. "Why couldn't it have been some mutt?"

Tom gave me a pitying look. "Criminals do predictable things. They follow patterns. We all do. But this crime doesn't match up with anything we've got—you know, the bashing on the head and then the suffocating. Whoever this was really wanted to make sure Friedman was dead. Anyhow, unless the perp commits another crime in the same style and gives us another crack at him, I doubt we'll go anywhere with this."

"Do you think maybe it was someone who hated her? From the way you talk about bashing and suffocating, it sounds that way."

He shrugged. "Could be."

"How about her brother?"

"He couldn't have done it. He also has a good alibi. Besides, what would he have gained from it? He was the beneficiary of her insurance policy, but it wasn't all that great. That little house she lived in wasn't even hers. She was renting. You want a beer?"

"Too early for me," I said. "I'll take a Coke, though, if you have one."

He said, "Sure," and left the room. As soon as he came back, I started with the questions again.

"Any other possibilities?" I asked.

"None that I know about. This looks like one of those dead-end cases, no pun intended. No conceivable motive and no likely perpetrator."

I laughed. "You sound like a detective on one of those TV shows."

"I don't watch them," he said, but I knew he wasn't telling the truth. It wasn't just needlepoint I'd caught him at. "Anyway, here's someone who's a real nice person, no enemies, and somebody kills her for no reason. What should we make of that?"

"I don't know," I said.

"Neither do the guys in Homicide. And don't try to find out."

I gave him my look of insulted innocence.

I could tell it didn't faze him. He knew I was like a hound on the scent of a fox when I get interested in working something out, and it was obvious that I was interested.

CHAPTER
5

I spent most of the rest of the week finishing two articles and sending out a bunch of query letters. Free-lance writers who don't hustle don't eat. Then I was ready to get started seriously on the Dilly Friedman piece.

On Thursday, I phoned Jim Cohen's office. His secretary said he was busy and would get back to me that day. He didn't. I rang him up again on Friday. This time the secretary kept me on hold a few minutes, then told me that Mr. Cohen was out of the office. She took a message. Why did I have a suspicion that Cohen wasn't going to return my call?

On Monday, I phoned Dilly's school and asked for permission to visit. I got it.

The school was in South Baltimore. It was an area I'd never visited, but I'd heard it was poor and run-down. I drove down Route 95 to Washington Boulevard, then turned off. I passed a scraggly line of one-story brown brick buildings that housed small businesses, things like car repair places and Laundromats.

Then I got to an area of projects, street after broken-down street of them. They were all brown brick, too, and ugly. Some of them had wash hanging outside. Some of them, the ones with boards on the windows, were empty. Quite a few of the boards had bullet holes through them.

Some of the windows did also. The place looked like a war zone where both sides had lost.

Scattered groups of men stood around on the pavement. A lot of them were smoking. Several of them appeared to be drinking stuff from brown paper bags, even though it was pretty early in the day. None of them seemed purposeful.

I pulled up to the school, which was across the street from another project with the same type of characters outside. There was a big sign above the wire covering the front door, the Nettie Blue School. I'd never heard of Nettie Blue and didn't know why something would be named after her. I'd also never heard of a school with wire in front of the door.

The school looked like a warehouse, big and ugly, with lots of windows. Most of the windows were painted over, I guess to stop the kids from looking out. There was wire mesh over the glass. I doubted it was to keep birds away.

I'm no coward, but when I got out of the car, I considered running. Groups of men with nothing to do make me nervous. I forced myself to walk.

I expected the inside of the school to be depressing, like the outside. Surprisingly, it wasn't. It was noisy, full of life, and, even with brown linoleum on every floor I could see, cheerful-looking. There were posters and uplifting signs stuck on the walls, things like YOU MAKE A DIFFERENCE. I went into the office and registered.

The principal was an attractive, well-dressed woman with light brown skin. She acted as though she was glad to see me. She made a phone call, then told me that someone would be up to escort me to Dilly's classroom.

My "escort" was a girl of about ten. I might have thought she was older because she already had a bustline, but the childishness of her face gave her away. It was a nice face, medium brown, with dark, steady eyes. Her brown hair was parted in the center and pulled back with a white twisty thing with a plastic ball on each end.

"I'm Rachel Crowne," I told the kid after we walked out of the office.

She didn't say anything.

I said, "What's your name?"

"Cleome."

Dilly had mentioned a Cleome. I doubted there was more than one because as a given name Cleome had to be rare. Chances were this was the kid. What had Dilly said about her, that she was smart but had trouble with math? "That's a pretty name," I said. "I guess your mom loves flowers, huh?"

She stared at me. "Why's that?"

"Cleome is a plant," I said. "It has pretty flowers."

"Oh yeah?"

This was rough going. "What's your last name, honey?"

"Hightower."

Before I could say anything, she said, "You think my mama like high towers?"

Score one for Miss Cleome.

We were going to the basement, and it seemed like the rest of the trip would be in silence. She walked ahead of me.

Her body was sturdy and big boned; it was serious looking. Her clothes were all right, I guess, but they looked old, and I saw that there was a hole in one sleeve. I would have bet that they'd been bought at the Goodwill.

We were almost at our destination when I stopped to examine some graffiti printed in uppercase letters on the wall. It said FOLK and FUK YU.

Cleome stopped, too. She turned her head toward the

scrawl. "That James can't spell for nothing," she said solemnly.

I grinned. "Maybe that's a good thing."

I don't know if it was my cool-dude attitude that did it, or what, but she lightened up a lot. Her smile was unexpectedly pleasant and mischievous. Shallow dimples flashed.

I figured she'd be a little more receptive now. "Was Miss Friedman one of your teachers?" I asked her.

The smile vanished. She nodded stiffly.

"Was she a good teacher?"

Again, the rigid nod.

I stopped and leaned against the wall. "You know she was killed. Do you have any idea why someone might have killed her?"

Cleome looked at me as though I were unsalvageably dumb. "Drugs," she said, drawing out the word as though it were a yard long.

Did this kid really know something? I doubted it, but just maybe this was a lead for the detective who had Dilly's case. I tried to keep my voice nonchalant. "Why do you say that?"

Again, I was bathed in scorn. "That's why people killed," she said. "They dealing in drugs, that's why. Everybody knows that. Unless they in gangs, and I don't think Miss Friedman was in no gangs."

She stopped suddenly.

"What is it?" I said.

"We're here."

Cleome pulled open the door to a large classroom that smelled of disinfectant and chalk. She showed me inside. I was pretty certain that was the end of our communication, meager as it had been.

The teacher was obviously expecting me. She was a lot friendlier than the kid. "I'm Iris Taylor," she said with a big smile and a handshake. "The principal told me you were coming down. She says you're going to write something about us. I hope it will be good."

"Sure," I said before glancing around the room. The front wall was taken up almost entirely by a blackboard. One half had math problems written on it. The other half had simple spelling words. The wall in the back had a long piece of white paper tacked up. At the top, the paper said GOOD-BYE, MISS FRIEDMAN. WE LOVE YOU. Scattered all over the sheet were painted figures of children, some dogs, a sun, and flowers.

"That's interesting," I said, and walked over to it. It was Elementary School Primitive. As I got close, I could see that in the center of the paper was a prone figure with blond hair. It had to be Dilly. There were a number of circles on the body, red stuff pouring out of them. In big print, the banner said SHOTTE!

Around the body were what I guessed were meant to be Ziploc bags and a pipe. The word next to them was DRUGS!

Beside each drawing of a child, there was a name. It wasn't a stretch to guess they were the names of Dilly's pupils.

I walked back to the teacher. Maybe Cleome's explanation for Dilly's death wasn't misleading. Maybe there was something to these kids' thinking she used drugs. "The police said Miss Friedman was suffocated, not shot, and I never heard she took or sold drugs. Why do these children think she did?"

"It's what they always think when someone dies," she said. "They're usually right. In Dilly's case, we didn't try to talk them out of it because we hoped it might be a lesson to them—though I doubt it." She pointed to one of the kids. "See him. That's Tony. He's nine. He's growing a long fingernail to use to scoop up cocaine."

"Nothing like being prepared," I said.

She was not amused. I didn't blame her.

"The kids seem to be different ages," I said. "How come?"

"This is a resource class. It gets pupils who need special help only in some of their subjects. That's what Dilly gave them." She sighed. "It's what I'll try to give them until they replace her. It's a difficult job. I don't know how Dilly did it and stayed so pleasant."

"Did you know her well?"

"Yes. I guess so."

"What was she like?"

"Nice," she said. "Really nice. She took her job seriously, but not too seriously, you know."

I didn't.

"You can't do too much for these kids. Most of them are hopeless cases. They've got a million strikes against them. They're bottomless pits of need. I could tell you stories. . . ." She shook her head. "A good teacher does what she can but doesn't let what she can't do get to her. That's how Dilly was."

"Can you tell my anything else?" I said. "Did she have any favorites that you know of?"

"If she did, it was that girl over there." She gestured toward Cleome.

Cleome stared at us. I had the feeling she'd been watching us during the whole conversation.

"Why her?" I asked.

"I don't know. She's a grim little thing. She doesn't talk or smile much. Of course, you can't blame her. Her mother is a crack addict and a prostitute. She neglects Cleome. Leaves her alone for days at a time. The kid doesn't know who her father is. Still, her situation is no worse than that of many of the other students."

The teacher looked at her watch. "It's almost lunch time,"

she said. "Did you know that ninety-eight percent of the kids here are eligible for free lunches? Ninety-eight percent! If it weren't for school, they wouldn't eat. This is not a country-club school. Dilly didn't mind, though. She loved the kids."

"Yes, that's what she told me the one time I talked to her."

The woman leaned closer. "Why do you think she was killed?"

"I haven't any idea. Can you tell me anything else about Dilly?"

She gave me more information, including a few anecdotes I knew I could use, and also filled me in on Dilly's students. She was right: they were bottomless pits of need.

"Would you mind if I handed out my card to the kids?" I said. "Maybe some of them would like to get in touch with me, tell me their stories about Dilly."

She looked doubtful. "Some of them don't have phones."

"They could write to me."

"Some of them can't write."

I was getting kind of annoyed. "Those who do have phones and can write can get in touch with me. I'm not going to worry about the others." I thought for a few seconds. "Does Cleome have a phone or anything?"

"Yes, I'm sure she does, because we call her mother when she doesn't come to school. That happens pretty frequently. The child has to take care of the mama."

If I'd come on a different day, I might not have met Cleome. The thought bothered me, though I didn't know why; we hadn't said more than a dozen words to each other, if that. Still, there was something about her. . . . Maybe it was simply her name.

"So, can I give out the cards?" I asked.

"Oh, certainly."

I made a little speech to the children about how I'd like to hear from them if they had anything to tell me about Miss Friedman. With some trepidation, I said they could call me collect.

Just as I was about to leave, Cleome walked over. She put her hand on my arm. "Ma'am . . . Miss Crowne, I'll be calling you," she said. "I got somethin' you might want to know about who murdered Miss Friedman."

CHAPTER
6

Several days went by without a phone call from even one of Dilly's kids. I was disappointed, especially at not hearing from Cleome. When she didn't get in touch, I figured she didn't know anything about the murder and had just been talking. Not that it mattered, of course; I probably had enough material for an article, and it wasn't my job to try to solve crimes.

By Friday, I gave up on the idea of waiting. I mailed off some business stuff, then decided to go to the Athletic Club. First, though, I needed to stop off at the Mall to exchange a pair of jeans.

I put on a blue short-sleeved knit shirt to soak up perspiration, a pair of jersey shorts, white socks, and white-and-blue running shoes. I started out the door, then turned back to collect my white sweatband. I was now ready for fifteen minutes of shopping and an hour or so of pain and torture at the club.

It was another fine-looking day. The sun was shining. The humidity was low. The haziness that often hung over this area was missing, and the sky was a lovely blue. It was a day for gardeners, like most of my neighbors. Unfortunately, I wasn't of their ilk. I loved flowers and green things; I just didn't want to plant and take care of them. When I walked outside, I admired the few blades of grass that struggled to prosper on my unwatered, untended lawn. I had to give them credit for their determination to survive under any odds.

Then I got in my old Toyota and took off, following Route 29 to the Mall. Everything looked fertile, gorgeous—and neat. Fairfield folks didn't tend to be litterers.

I wondered how such a calm, pretty place could harbor a murderer. But apparently it did, and he hadn't been caught yet. Was he apprehensive, or did he think he was really slick and was going to get away with it?

Remembering Dilly, and the kids who needed her, I felt a jolt of anger. If I could do anything to nail him, I would.

Our main mall is a two-story structure in the heart of Fairfield, consisting of a central block anchored by a department store at each end and two wings. Though enclosed, its vaulted glass roof lets light inside. The Mall is a nice place to shop, except that's something I rarely do. I probably spend more time at the food court stalls than at any of the retail stores.

The stalls were pretty close to the main entrance. I could smell some of their wares when I walked in: roast turkey, pizza, lamb gyros, Chinese food, coffee, and fresh tomato sauce. I promised myself a return visit after I exercised. If I ate before, I'd get sick.

I was headed toward The Gap to return the jeans when I saw Mrs. Pearl, the woman who'd eulogized Dilly at the memorial service. She was staring into Brookstone's window, apparently gazing at a fan. I had a feeling, though, that she really didn't see it.

She was dressed in a rather fussy long-sleeved yellow dress, very different from what she'd worn at the service. It seemed more in keeping with the personality she projected than the other, more somber dress. As before, however, she had a blanket over her legs, this one a tan, cashmere-looking affair. She turned her chair toward me, and I saw that her light brown eyes were still ringed with deep circles as though she suffered a lot and didn't sleep. I found myself feeling sorry for her all over again.

I don't think she recognized me at first. As I walked toward her, I could see exactly when she figured out who I was. Her face lit up with a smile and she extended her hands. "How are you, dear?" she said.

I told her I was fine, then asked her the same question. I got the same answer, but I didn't believe it. She wheeled a bit closer. "Do you have time for sharing some coffee with me?"

"Sure," I said, "but I'll make mine Evian water."

I had to explain to her that I wasn't a health fanatic or a Seventh-Day Adventist and was abstaining only because exercise and food, especially food containing caffeine, didn't mix well. She gave me an accepting smile, led me to a Starbucks, and insisted on treating me to the Evian.

We found a table near the main fountain, and I put down the drinks. "It's so nice seeing you again," she said. "In fact, I've been planning to call you."

"Is that so?"

"Oh yes. I think we have a lot in common. I don't mean just Dilly and an interest in finding out who murdered her, but a concern for the education of children."

"Sure," I said. "Tell me, who do you think killed Dilly?"

She put down her cup. A little of the coffee spilled into the saucer. "I don't know. Do you?"

"Her students think she was killed for being a drug dealer."

Mrs. Pearl said, "That's the most ridiculous thing I've ever heard. Dilly would no more sell drugs than I would."

"I agree," I said, "but to kids like that drugs are a reasonable explanation for violence."

"I guess so. The children I work with are different. Fairfield isn't South Baltimore."

"It certainly isn't."

She tilted her head, making me think of a small, fragile bird. "I know you're interested in Dilly, and there are so many things I can tell you."

"That's great," I said. "How would you describe her nature?"

"She was very sweet."

"Yes, you said that at the memorial service. Do you have any examples that would show that?"

"Why, yes. You heard the rabbi talk about the Delilah thing, how she never let her mother know she'd done something silly."

I nodded. "I'd like to hear one of your stories, if you can think of one."

Her fingers fluttered. "Let me see. I met Dilly by accident, you might say. I bumped into her and my son here, in this very mall. They were holding hands and laughing. They looked so darling together."

She gazed at me expectantly. I didn't know what she wanted from me, so I didn't react at all.

"Naturally, I was surprised because Everett had never mentioned to me that he was going with anyone. We were very close, so that's something I would have expected. When I came upon them, he blushed and dropped her hand. Everett is shy and proper, not like so many of the young people you see now."

"That's nice to hear," I said, wondering if the story was going anywhere.

She sighed. "He was always concerned with my feelings. At any rate, we three had lunch together. I must confess I found Dilly a little colorful—one might even say flamboyant—but I could see she was right for him. She brought him out."

I couldn't deny that Dilly was colorful, and I could picture her being a good foil for a shy person. I nodded.

"That's what I wanted to tell you. Dilly had the ability to enhance Everett's personality. She was right for him." She paused. "Did I say that before? Well, she was."

The pain lines deepened. I waited. "How could I not like her?" she asked as though my answer would be important. "A mother has to have positive feelings for a girl who loves her son."

I could have argued with that. I had loved my first husband, at least before I found out that he lacked loyalty. But his mother couldn't stand me from the get-go. She didn't like the way I dressed, talked, thought—you name it. When she found out that I was unable to get pregnant, she said she'd always known it.

There was no point in contradicting Mrs. Pearl, though. I told her I agreed with her.

She went on. "After that, I invited her to my house for Sunday tea a number of times. We became more like friends than future mother- and daughter-in-law. Then, after Everett died, we continued our friendship."

I could understand how mutual grief would bind them together. I nodded.

"Now that Dilly's gone . . ." Her voice broke. I waited. She sniffed a few times, then said, "Did I tell you I've decided to establish a foundation in both their names, as a memorial? Well, I have. I'm not without means. My daddy left me financially secure. I've been thinking and thinking about it, and just last night I determined I would do it. This foundation will provide scholarships for graduating high school seniors who want to major in art or art history in college. Everett was an artist, you know."

"That's very nice," I said, although I couldn't see how her idea would be a memorial to Dilly's concerns. I thought it would have been better to create something that would help Baltimore inner-city kids express their artistic leanings. It wasn't my money, though, so I kept my mouth shut.

Mrs. Pearl said, "Would you like to see Everett's picture?" Without waiting for an answer, she pulled a big yellow leather purse out from under the blanket and delved into it. "Here," she said, her voice a mixture of pride and pain. "This is Everett."

He seemed awfully young, which, of course, he had been when he died. He wasn't unattractive, except that he was too thin. Wisps of dark hair hung over his eyebrows. His eyes were large and brown and ringed with thick lashes. I think it was his eyes that gave him such a vulnerable look.

I happen to believe that always telling the truth is a vastly overrated virtue. I returned the picture and said, "He was very handsome."

Mrs. Pearl inhaled as though it hurt to do it. "He was, wasn't he? Everybody loved him."

"Did you tell me that he and Dilly were already engaged when he died?" I prompted.

"Yes, they were. If his accident hadn't happened, I'd have a son and grandchildren now. Instead, I have nothing."

What could I say?

"What did Dilly do after he died?" I asked.

"She grieved, of course, and remained true to him. That's why she never married. Theirs was a real love. It would have lasted, not like these arrangements most young people now have. They usually don't go past the first anniversary."

Maybe that was the explanation for Dilly's lack of involvement with other people. I didn't understand why her brother hadn't thought of it. On the other hand, he'd said she'd had a boyfriend, Murray somebody. That fact contradicted what Etta told me.

She said, "What are you thinking?"

I could have told her, but I didn't want to put her on the spot. That would be like kicking a wounded animal. I said, "I was wondering why you rented your house to her."

She returned the photo to her purse and put the purse under the blanket again. "As you know, she taught. She didn't make much. That's why I rented my house to her. One must do things to help other people."

"That's very nice of you."

"A Jew who doesn't perform *tsadakah* isn't a worthy person."

Right. Honor your father and mother and give to help those less fortunate. Anything else came after those, in my opinion.

"I made the rent cheap. I guess I felt I owed her something for almost having been my son's wife. You can understand that, can't you?"

I nodded, then asked, "When did your son die?"

Her face seemed to crumple. I thought she might cry, but she didn't. She sat straighter in her chair. "He died a week or so after graduation; I never can remember the exact . . . It was an accident."

"Car wreck?" I said, wondering if it was also the explanation for her paralysis.

She shook her head. A blond-gray curl moved forward

and touched her cheek. She swiped it toward the back of her head.

"It was his dentist's fault," she said. "After Everett had his wisdom teeth extracted, he developed something called dry socket. The pain was terrible. The dentist gave him pain pills, but they didn't help. So he took more. He took too many. Of course, he didn't know what he was doing. The pain confused him, you see. That's what the coroner said. Finally, the pills killed him; he stopped breathing." Her voice trailed away. "It was an accident."

"I'm sorry."

She dabbed at her eyes. "I'm always sorry. Every day."

More to change the subject than for any other reason, I said, "Did your son major in special education, too? Is that how he met Dilly?"

"Everett? No indeed. He majored in fine arts. He had prodigious talent. Everyone recognized it. When he died, the world lost Leonardo da Vinci all over again."

I took that with a grain of salt. My mother was convinced that, given time, I would outshine Pavlova; instead, despite all my years of ballet lessons, I never did show any talent.

"Tell me about the Six-Pack," I said. "I know they included Dilly, your son, Jim Cohen, and the Reverend McCauley. Who were the others?"

She looked surprised. "We talked about that before. Why do you still want to know about them? They're past history, dear."

"I'm interested in them because they can tell me what Dilly was like when she was younger."

She gave me a doubtful look. "I suppose so. Unfortunately, I can't remember the names. . . . My memory comes and goes. I guess I'm getting old." I didn't say anything. She added, "If I do remember, I'll call you and let you know. Would that be all right?"

Damn, I wanted those names. I said, "Are you and Jim Cohen friends?"

She seemed amused. "Hardly. I don't think he has an artistic bone in his body. I know him, that's all. Lots of people do."

"Yes. We spoke after the memorial service."

"Really? What did he say about Everett?"

"He said he was sensitive."

She looked at me sadly. "Yes. He had the spirit of a true artist. Like you, Rachel."

Me? I wrote articles. I wasn't Saul Bellow. I wondered if she was buttering me up. If she was, I couldn't imagine why.

I must have looked skeptical.

She said in a kind voice, "Don't doubt yourself, dear."

That sort of annoyed me. I didn't doubt myself, but I didn't inflate my talents, either. What I did was try, to the best of my ability, to be as fair and objective as possible about my capabilities. That's how I knew I wasn't another Saul Bellow. I wasn't going to argue with her, though, or explain how I thought; it wasn't worth it to me. "Sure," I said. "Look, I'd really like to know who the others were. If you think of their names, will you call me?"

She sighed. "I'll try. Would that be all right?"

"Certainly. I'd be grateful."

Her right hand went to the buttons on her wheelchair. "I've got to go now."

She started to move away from me. Then she stopped. I got up and walked toward her. "Is anything wrong?"

"Dicky Miller," she said. "He's the one with all the hair. He drives a local bus here in Fairfield. But I swear that's the only other one I can remember. Why don't you ask Jim Cohen?"

"I will," I said. "I definitely will—if he ever calls me back."

"Why wouldn't he want to?"

"That's a good question. I'll let you know if I learn the answer."

"Yes, please. Do that." She reached over, grabbed my hand, and squeezed it. "I want to find out who did this. I really do."

CHAPTER
7

"Who is it?" I yelled, wishing the person on the other side of the door would stop ringing the bell. It was Saturday morning. I wanted to sleep, not socialize.

"It's me," a voice I didn't recognize answered.

"Who's me?" I said, and looked through the peephole.

There stood a young brown-skinned girl, her dark hair divided into a number of sections, each one held together with a brightly colored piece of elastic with a round plastic ball on the end. I flung the door open. "Cleome, what are you doing here?"

"Said I had something to tell you. Couldn't get to your place before now."

"Come on in. What's that thing?" I pointed to the huge radio she was carrying.

She held it up. It was ugly, with about a million knobs. "That's my boom box," she said proudly. "One of my mama's friends just give it to me."

"Very nice, but why did you bring it here? I have a radio."

She put down the box, then spread her hands, palms up. "Can't leave it home."

I had a good idea what wasn't being said—that it would be stolen if she did. What a life this kid must have, I thought.

"Okay, fine. But shouldn't you have called me?"

"You want me to leave?"

"No, silly. I didn't mean that. If you'd phoned to let me know you planned to visit, I would have driven into Baltimore and gotten you." I looked around. I didn't see anybody else. "Did your mother bring you?"

"Nah."

"Then how did you get here?"

"Hitched," she said matter-of-factly.

"Hitched?" I echoed, then closed the door. "Don't you know how dangerous that can be? Didn't Miss Friedman teach you that?"

"She taught me. She said, 'Cleome, don't never take a ride, or anything else, from a man. Men can't be trusted.' So I didn't. I got a ride with a woman. Little white lady like you."

That advice didn't sound like it came from the Dilly I knew about. It sounded like it was from someone who'd been badly burned at the fires of love. I frowned. "Why did she say that?"

"You got a drink?" Cleome said. "I'm thirsty."

I took her into the kitchen and seated her on a chair. I poured her some milk. Then I began making her a roast beef sandwich. "Mayonnaise or mustard?" I asked.

"For what?"

"For your sandwich."

"Didn't ask for no sandwich."

Maybe she hadn't, but I could see from her expression that she was hungry. I remembered Dilly's schoolteacher friend saying that 98 percent of the kids at the school got free lunches because they needed them. I put mayonnaise on one piece of bread and mustard on the other. Then I made a peanut-butter-and-jelly sandwich and gave her that, too. She ate every crumb. I set a package of Tastykake chocolate cupcakes in front of her and poured her more milk.

Cleome took two bites out of a cupcake, then started to laugh.

"What is it?" I said.

She pointed to the cupcake. The marks of her front teeth were clearly imprinted on the soft icing. "That's funny," she said.

I laughed with her. In fact, I felt happy. Probably it was my Jewish hospitality genes expressing themselves, but, whatever, feeding the kid gave me a lot of pleasure.

She finished her second glass of milk and the remaining cupcakes, then sat back with a sigh. She folded her hands over her belly and looked at me. "Why you wearing those clothes?" she said.

"What clothes? These are my pajamas. I was in bed when you knocked." The pajamas in question were a red-and-white-striped shortie outfit I'd had since under-graduate school and washed about two thousand times. The white stripes were now yellowish, the red ones an anemic pink, and there was a hole in the shirt where I'd caught it on a nail. I loved the set and planned on wearing it for several more years.

"You can get clothes at the Goodwill," Cleome said. "Or some of the churches. I got this"—she pointed to her orange cotton dress, missing a belt—"at the flea market near my house. My mama paid plenty for it. It don't have no holes at all."

I had a feeling that she wasn't telling the truth about where she got the dress. This child was proud; I could see that. I said, "Thank you for the information."

"You're welcome." She pushed a couple of crumbs around with her left hand, then looked up at me. "What am I going to call you?" she said. "You like Aunt Crowne?" She pronounced "aunt" as "auhnt."

I grimaced.

"What's the matter? You want me to call you something else?"

"It's not that," I said, sitting down across from her and steepling my fingers together. "It's that I don't say 'auhnt.' I say 'ant'—you know, like the little bug."

Cleome said, "I ain't going to call you no ant. You better pick something else."

"You called Dilly Friedman 'Miss Friedman.' "

"Course I did. She was my teacher. You're not."

I grinned. "Okay. How about Rachel, or Miss Rachel, if you're more comfortable with that?"

"I'll call you Miss Rachel."

We shook hands on it.

Suddenly serious, she said, "Anybody know yet who killed Miss Friedman?"

I shook my head.

"You want to hear what I got to say about her? Maybe it will help."

I nodded, equally serious.

"She say, 'Men're no good. They're all pigs. If they're not at first, they will be later.' "

"Why would she say that?" I wondered out loud.

"Don't know." Cleome raised her square shoulders. "She say, 'Men be the death of me.' Now you know it was men killed her."

How do you explain to a ten-year-old kid that not everything should be taken literally? "Any particular men?" I asked. "Did she talk about a boyfriend?"

"Miss Friedman, she don't have no boyfriend. She told me she don't want one. Used to have lots in college, she say, but not no more."

Something had certainly happened between the time she'd left school and the time she'd talked to Cleome. I wondered if she'd been jilted. I doubted she'd have

sounded so bitter—and passed that bitterness on to a
child—because a boyfriend had accidently overdosed, so
I didn't think Everett Pearl's death could have been the
cause of her bleak view of the other sex. Maybe Murray
Rothman, the only guy I'd heard about her dating since
college, was at fault.

"When did she say those things to you?" I asked.

Cleome belched gently behind her hand. I wondered if
I'd overfed her. "All the time," she said. "When we're
alone. When I visit."

"Do you mean you used to go to her house?"

Cleome said yes.

"Did your mother ever object?"

"Uh-uh."

"Tell me about your mother," I said.

She stared at me suspiciously. "Why you want to know
about her? She don't have nothing to do with Miss
Friedman being killed."

"I didn't think she did," I said. "You don't have to if
you don't want to."

"I guess I can tell you something. She's nice."

A crack addict, prostitute, and absentee mom didn't
sound nice to me. When my mother left me, it was
because she was dead; nothing else could have made her
go. I almost asked if she was sure about her mother's
niceness but stopped myself. My face probably showed
what I was thinking, though. Cleome said, "She's as nice
as she's able to be, don't you know. She's got problems."

I waited, but apparently she had no intention of being
more specific.

"Will she mind that you're here?"

"Nah, she don't even know. She's not home. Maybe
she'll come back tomorrow, maybe not."

"Tomorrow? But where will you sleep tonight?"

"Home, I guess. Where else I going to go?"

"You can't stay there alone. You're only ten."

She shrugged. "You want me to stay here tonight?"

Did I? You bet I did, even as I entertained the suspicion that Cleome had worked all this out ahead of time. She had street smarts. That was nothing against her. If she hadn't, she probably wouldn't have survived to ten.

"If you want to," I said, hoping I sounded as casual as she did. Actually, I was excited. I was going to get a chance to play mother, a role I'd never have in real life, apparently. "I can take you home tomorrow night, if that's all right."

She grinned. "Might be all right for me if I'm lucky. Not so good for you, Miss Rachel."

"Why not?"

" 'Cause somebody might take it in mind to shoot you. Could happen."

"Okay," I said. "Is tomorrow afternoon okay?"

"It is if your car don't break down."

That was some place where she lived. All I said, though, was "Great." I started to offer her more food but decided I was being ridiculous. I'd wait a half hour or so. "Come on in the living room," I said.

When she sat on the sofa, she looked around, her eyes checking out the two old armchairs, the tables that didn't match, and the books, which were everywhere. "Miss Friedman's place is nicer," she said.

"Cleome, why do you think someone killed her?"

"Drugs." Like last time, she drew out the word.

"Nope. Something else. Perhaps one of those men she said shouldn't be trusted."

"Don't know," she said. "How're we going to find out?"

"We?"

"Yes, ma'am. That's why I come."

CHAPTER
8

Naturally, I had no intention of putting Cleome in danger. Or myself. I valued my skin, too. This would be strictly an intellectual venture, to be worked out on paper. But how to go about it?

I decided that the first thing we should do was to be brought up to date by my friend Tom. "Let's go talk to the guy next door," I said. "He's a policeman here in the county. He'll know if anything new is happening on the case."

She backed off, her face set. "Ain't going to talk to no cop."

"Cleome, why not?"

She looked at me as though I were an idiot. "I ain't talking to no cop."

"But, he's not just a policeman. He's my friend and neighbor."

"Don't care if he's living in this house and he's your brother. I ain't talking to him."

I guess I should have expected her to be like that. But I wanted Cleome to trust Tom.

We argued a little bit, but the argument came to an end when the phone rang; I was glad, because I was losing. To my surprise and hers, the call was for Cleome. "I've got to go home," she said after hanging up. "That was Miss Betty, my mama's friend. I gave her your number just in case of something. She said my mama came back already, and she needs me."

I tried to hide my disappointment. "I'll drive you," I said in what I hoped was a neutral tone of voice. She nodded.

"Is your mother all right?"

"She ain't feeling too good. Sometime that happens."

Since I had an idea of Mama's lifestyle, that was no surprise to me. "Does she need to go to the hospital? I could take her."

My offer was turned down, as was my suggestion that I provide Cleome with a brown-bag lunch. "You think we don't got food," she said. "We do. My mama got an Independence card."

She had to translate for me. It seemed that, in Maryland at least, food stamps had been replaced by a card that could be used instead of cash or stamps at grocery stores. "Can't buy no toilet paper or paper towels, though," she said. "If you can't eat it, you ain't going to get it."

"I've got extras of both," I said. "How about if I give you some?"

"No thanks."

"For your mother."

"My mother? Well, maybe that would be all right."

Cleome was proud. I needed to remember that.

I drove her to her house, taking Route 95, then going through the same ugly, frightening streets I'd followed when I visited the Nettie Blue School. They looked even worse to me this time because I knew this was where Cleome lived. She had a hundred strikes against her; probably all the people who had to stay there did.

I gave her the items for her mama, then left her; her neighborhood wasn't someplace I wanted to hang around anyway, unless I had an armed guard with me. The only thing that made me feel better was that she gave me her number and promised to call me the following Saturday so that I could pick her up. On the way home, I planned the meals I would make for her.

As I drove onto my street, I saw that Tom's unmarked wasn't there. Full of energy, on which I now had nothing to expend it, I decided to track down the local bus driver who'd been one of the Six-Pack. A call to the company, along with a story about being his long-lost cousin who had to see him right away, got me his route. All I needed to do was intercept him.

This I did by driving to one of his stops and waiting until his bus showed up. "Are you Dicky Miller?" I asked before offering him my money.

He gave me a big, friendly grin. "Yeah, man, that's me. What up?"

He had been to college, but he sounded like one of the kids at Cleome's school. He didn't look like any of them, though. For one thing, he was white. For another, he didn't appear as well-groomed.

Miller was of medium height and skinny, with dark hair that reached his shoulders, dark eyes, a narrow face, and a scraggly brown beard. Except for the grin and a cheerful manner that seemed ingrained, he would have looked scary, like Charlie Manson.

He was wearing a black leather vest over a black T-shirt, black leather pants, black boots, and a lot of silver-colored stuff—a belt, bracelets, and spurs—that kept jingling. He smelled strongly of cigarettes. In any other community, given his appearance, I doubted he'd have gotten the job he had. However, Fairfield was still liberal and small enough to tolerate outliers like Dicky, not to mention the fact that the company probably paid him next to nothing.

I wondered what he'd majored in in college. Somehow, I didn't think it was bus driving.

"I wanted to talk to you about Dilly Friedman," I said.

The bus swerved, and a teenager sitting on a seat in the third row yelled, "Hey, watch it, asshole."

"Let's talk after I get through my run," Dicky said, no longer smiling, and I agreed.

I took a seat in the back and watched Fairfield go by. It really was an attractive place, full of nice, if uninventive, mostly pseudocolonial houses, green lawns, and bright flower beds. What I especially liked were the wide swaths of red and purple wildflowers that had been seeded in the open spaces. Pretty Fairfield—where a person had put a plastic bag over Dilly's head so that she would die. Was the killer laughing because he'd bested the police so far, or was he scared? Had he just been after Dilly, or did he have plans to kill someone else here? And what was the motive for the murder?

After about twenty minutes, nobody was on the bus but Dicky Miller and me. He pulled over to a vacant lot, opened the front double doors, and lit a cigarette. "So you want to talk about Dilly," he said after I moved up to a seat near him. "Are you a five-oh?"

"A what?"

"You know—a five-oh. A cop. Don't you speak English?"

"I hope so. I'm a writer. I'm writing an article about Dilly and the kids she taught. She did a good job, and I thought her experiences would make an interesting story. Even though she's dead, I'd like to finish the article."

I added, "I saw you at her memorial service."

He inhaled deeply on his cigarette, then let the smoke out slowly, as though the cylinder were filled with pot. He flicked ash on the floor, then looked over at me belligerently. "So, why are you interviewing me? A lot of people were there. How do you even know who I am, for Christ's sake?"

"Mrs. Pearl told me—you know, Everett's mother. She said you and Dilly used to be friends."

"Yeah? I didn't think she knew about that. Ev didn't like to tell her much. She was too interested in getting into his business. In fact, I think she thought he was still a little boy."

When I didn't say anything in response, he said, "Ev's dead, you know."

"Yes, his mother told me. She said it was an accidental death. He OD'd on pain pills."

"I heard that. It's funny."

Maybe there was something wrong with my sense of humor. "Funny?"

"I don't mean like a joke. I mean strange. He was never into drugs."

"Was Dilly?"

"Not her. She didn't even drink much, which was just as well because she couldn't hold her liquor. At first we thought she was just putting it on, you know, but that's really how she was."

I pictured her, the wide mouth smeared with lipstick, blond hair falling over her face. She wouldn't make an attractive drunk, if there were such a thing.

As though he were reading my mind, Dicky said, "She was a sloppy drunk. Two beers and she'd be on the floor with her skirt up to her you-know-what."

"Good thing she had friends like you to protect her."

"Right."

I said, "Look, all I want is to ask you a few questions about when you and Dilly were in school together. I'm trying to fill in a background on her. Was there anything about her then that would have made you think she'd make a terrific teacher?"

He laughed. "Dilly? The ditz brain? Nah."

I didn't like his making negative remarks about her. "If you thought so little of her, why did you go to her memorial service?"

"I didn't think little of her. What makes you say that? Anyway, it was Jim Cohen's idea to go to the service. He's running for some kind of political job."

"Are you telling me that's why he went?"

Miller grinned. "Could be."

"But you're not running for office, are you?"

"Meaning what?"

"Meaning why were you there?"

"I didn't have anything else to do, not that it's your business. Besides, I like getting together with my old friends once in a while, as long as it's not too often."

I must have had a disapproving look on my face because he said, "What's eating you?"

"You sound as though Dilly's death didn't matter to you. Is that true?"

"Well, sure it mattered. I liked her. To tell you the truth, though, I hadn't seen her for years."

"Not since when?"

He squirmed in his seat. "Not since graduation night. What is this, the third degree? Why are you asking all these questions?"

"I told you why."

"Yeah, says you. Are you sure you're not investigating her murder? Maybe that's what you're really writing about."

"I'm not," I said, "but suppose I were. How would that involve you?"

"That's what I'm saying. It wouldn't."

He dropped the cigarette, then picked it up and pitched it out the door. "Look, I was practically blown away when I heard about her death. You don't expect people you know to be murdered, or die for any reason at our age." As he said this, he took hold of a strand of his hair and began rubbing it between the thumb and first finger of his right hand. I had seen little kids do that when they needed comforting. Well, why not? Unless he'd killed her, he would have been shocked about her death. Also, he had gone to school with her, and he had been her friend.

"When did the murder happen?" he asked.

"About a week and a half ago, on a Saturday night."

He looked relieved. "I wasn't here. I had a gig in Colorado; I got back this past Thursday."

His relief struck me as odd. I wondered if he'd worried about being implicated and, if so, why. Maybe he was a guilty type. I'd met a few like that. I decided not to comment on his odd reaction. "You mentioned a gig," I said. "Are you a musician?"

"Drums. I'm doing this until I get discovered." The grin was on his face again.

I said, "Tell me more about you and Dilly."

I noticed two thin lines of sweat making patterns under his T-shirt. I found myself wondering if the vest made him hot. The only leather I'd ever worn was in shoes and purses. Or was it my question that caused him to perspire?

"What do you mean?" he said, raising his voice. "I liked her, like I said, but she was never my woman, if that's what you're getting at. We were a bunch of friends, see, not just me and her. There were six of us."

His loud voice didn't intimidate me, as it was obviously meant to do, but I didn't like it. "Yes, I heard that."

"Who from? Mrs. Pearl again?"

I shrugged, then said, "Who was the other guy in the

Six-Pack? I can only account for five of you, including Dilly."

His eyebrows went up, making two dark peaks on his tanned forehead. "Why do you need to know? That doesn't have anything to do with teaching, does it?"

What I wanted to know was why I was having a hard time getting all six names. I said, "It has to do with her life. That's what I want to learn about. It's what I want to ask people, as many people as I can who knew her." He looked unconvinced. "She was a good person, Dicky. I want to share that with others."

He hesitated, then said, "If that's how you get your excitement, far be it from me to put obstacles in your way. Okay. She was nice. She had a neat sense of humor, and she didn't expect anything special because she was a girl. She paid for herself, and she wasn't always whining and bitching, like so many do. What else do you need?"

"The name of the sixth person."

"You're a pain in the butt," he said, "but I'll tell you. You know why? I don't want you going away believing I have anything to hide, because I don't. The Six-Pack was her, me, Ev, Jimbo Cohen—you know who he is?" I nodded. "He was always slick. I met him in a freshman math class. Actually, we didn't have much in common, but we stayed friends." He shrugged his thin shoulders. "I don't know why, because I never liked him much."

I could believe the part about them not having much in common. James Cohen, running for office, wasn't likely to hang around a type like Dicky Miller, no matter what their past association. "When was the last time you saw him?"

"Besides the service? I don't know. What's the difference?"

"I'm curious. It's a writer's occupational disease."

"Is it? I only know musicians . . . and bus drivers.

Which reminds me—I'd better bring this bus back or my supervisor will have a fit. So get off."

"Just a couple more questions?"

"This isn't my problem."

"Please?"

He shrugged. "Make it quick."

He reached under his black shirt and scratched his chest. I wondered if it was hard for the Fairfield bus manager to get drivers.

"What do you know about Bob McCauley, the guy who recited a poem at the service?"

Dicky Miller began to laugh. "He's a minister."

"Why is that humorous?"

"Why not?"

"You tell me."

"Okay. You expect a minister to be a really decent guy, don't you? Good morals and like that?"

"I guess so. Isn't he?"

"Not decent enough. He's got sins on him—if you believe that kind of stuff. Personally, I don't. What's done is over, if you get my meaning. It's the past. You can't change it, so forget it. That's how I feel."

"Tell me what this McCauley should forget? Did any of it have to do with Dilly?"

Dicky turned the key in the ignition. The heavy sound of a bus motor filled the air. "You better get off the bus," he said. "I've got to get back."

He stood up and began shoving at me, little shoves, not exactly threatening, not yet. Still, I wasn't sure that he wouldn't kick me off if I didn't move. Before he closed the doors, I said, "Who was the sixth member of the Pack?"

The doors shut with a whoosh of air, and he drove off. Damn, I thought. What's going on? And how am I supposed to get back to where I parked my car?

CHAPTER
9

I got a call from Jordan Goldman, my sort-of boy-friend, the day after I talked with Dicky Miller. He'd been home from Florida for about twelve hours.

"I missed you," he said.

"Oh, were you away?"

"That's what I like about you, honey. You always stroke my ego."

Even though we were teasing each other, I was very much aware that he'd said he *liked* me. He was a mathe-matician. Being precise was important to him. If he said "like," he didn't mean "love."

He laughed and asked if he could come over. I said sure.

A half hour later he was there, without his children. That was something. It wasn't that I didn't care for them. In fact, I was crazy about them and wished they were mine. I had a strong feeling, though, that they would never be. They came as a package with their father, and the odds of attaching him on a permanent basis didn't seem in my favor so far.

Jordan was a dark-haired, nice-looking guy, but now, with a deep tan, he was gorgeous. He was about six three, which made him a foot taller than I was, with a strongly molded face and muscled body, both of which reminded me of Michelangelo's statue of David. If there was ever a prime example of a sound mind in a sound body, he was it.

He was wearing a short-sleeved blue shirt, dark blue slacks, and running shoes with white socks. The hairs on his arms were tipped with gold from the sun. He smelled warm and musky, like semitropical places.

"Kiss me," he said when he came in, and I did. Then he did. Then we went into the bedroom and fell onto the bed. In no time at all, we were naked and making love.

Afterward, as I lay there next to him, I said, "What are you thinking about?" I almost always said that afterward.

He rubbed his foot along the length of my leg. "Nothing." That was something he almost always said, too. Jordan was smart but he wasn't much for sharing his thoughts.

"I'm thinking about something," I told him. "I'm making up a bumper sticker for my car: Do it with a mathematician; it always adds up."

He appeared to consider this, with an expression as serious as though I'd asked him for the solution to a problem in differential equations. "That's not bad. How about this: Statisticians do it better on average."

"We're not doing bumper stickers about statisticians."

"Oh."

I laughed, and he tousled my hair. That's something I've always disliked. It wasn't so bad when he did it, though. I could love this guy big-time, I thought. Then I felt sad because unrequited love, which is probably no more than it would turn out to be in this situation, is absurd in a thirty-five-year-old lady.

It wasn't that Jordan was grieving for his ex-wife. She'd divorced him several years before she was killed and was engaged to someone else when it happened. It was because of the kids. Although the three-year-old appeared to have gotten over her mother's death pretty nicely, the one aged five, a handsome little boy, had been a basket case. He was just starting to come out of his shell. I knew that, if necessary, Jordan would devote uninterrupted years to healing his son. No woman was going to sidetrack him. That's how Jordan was. I both admired and didn't care for that about him.

No use crying over milk that hadn't spilled yet, I told myself. I said, "A woman I know was murdered while you were away."

He blinked at the quick change of topic, then gave me a suspicious look. "Yes?"

I knew what his expression signified. It meant he was worried that I would get involved, as I'd done when his ex-wife was murdered.

"She was a teacher in Baltimore," I said. "I was doing an article on her."

He shrugged. "I guess now you can't do it."

"Yes, I can. I mean, I did. It's just about finished. Maybe I'll give it one more polish."

"And then?"

"Then Nancy is going to publish it."

"Ah, Nancy. How is the . . . ?"

I put my hand over his mouth. "Don't say it. She's my friend."

I don't know why Jordan and Nancy didn't like each other. I thought both of them were terrific. She disliked Tom Brant, too. Could she be jealous? That isn't something I'd ever suggest to her.

"What are you going to do next?" Jordan asked.

"You mean, besides try to find out who killed her?"

"No, you're not."

Actually, I hadn't made up my mind that I was going to do it, other than as a pen-and-paper exercise, as I'd told Cleome. I said that because I wanted to find out how far he'd go to stop me from endangering myself. I guess I'm not as grown up as I like to think I am.

"Oh yes, I am," I said.

He gave me a disapproving look but didn't say anything else.

I waited.

He said, "What's the name of this woman who was killed?"

"Dilly Friedman."

"Jewish, huh?"

"Yes, she was. And nice."

"Tell me about it."

I did.

"I know I shouldn't encourage you, but I'm curious. Do you have any idea about who could have done it, or why?"

"I'm betting on one of the Six-Pack."

Naturally, this drew a blank look.

"I'll tell you about them," I said, "but would you mind if I take a shower first?"

"I'll take one with you."

He did, and this led to that, and we were in the shower a long time. After we dried off and got dressed, I stifled my yawns and made us some sandwiches. Whereas sex makes me sleepy, it made Jordan hungry.

"Tell me about the Six-Pack," he said after swallowing a big bite of vegetable salad with Tabasco on rye. Jordan was a vegetarian with an insatiable lust for spicy food.

"I know the names of five. Dilly was one of them. They were part of her past. They were all buddies in college. After she graduated, she stopped making friends. I just wonder if something happened between her and the others to change her so much."

"Even if it did, so what? How would it relate to her being murdered?"

"That's a good question," I said. "Truthfully, I think I'm interested in them because I haven't heard of anyone else in her life who meant something to her after that. If I don't concentrate on them, there isn't anybody else to go after as far as I know. Well, there is one person," I said, reconsidering, "but my hunch is that he's not important."

"I see your point about this Six-Pack, though I don't like the going-after business. When did she graduate?"

"Five years ago."

"Let's assume something did happen back then. Why would anyone wait five years to kill her?"

"Beats me."

I could see that, despite himself, he was getting genuinely interested. Problem solving was what he liked best. "All right," he said. "Suppose it was one of those people. Are they all men?"

"All but Dilly."

"Okay. Let's say something happened in college, or after, between Dilly and one of them. That's what you're thinking."

"It's a possibility."

"We have to consider why there would be that gap of five years."

"Suppose whatever the thing was, it just happened," I said.

"Maybe. But you've been thinking that it happened in the past and changed her."

"That's true. So this might have been the first time he was in danger of exposure."

Jordan stared thoughtfully at me. "Do you think she was blackmailing someone?"

"I suppose she could have been, but I don't think she was the type."

"Well, maybe whatever happened before didn't matter because he didn't have anything to lose. Now he does."

"That could be." I took a deep breath. "Or maybe he's been mad all this time but just lost control of himself. So he hit her over the head and then suffocated her with a plastic bag. What do we do now?"

Jordan frowned at me. "If we were doing anything, we'd find out if something happened five years ago, what it was, and how these people would be affected by its disclosure. *But*"—he emphasized the word—"but, I'm not going to do anything. And you're not going to do anything. It's not our business. It's the business of the police. I'm sure they're working on it."

"The five-ohs," I said.

"What?"

"Nothing."

"Do you understand what I'm saying, honey?"

"Sure," I said.

"Yes, sure. You don't fool me, Rachel Crowne. You're listening, but you're not absorbing a thing I've said. You need to. Whoever killed her is just as capable of killing you. And will, if you get in his way. This is a ruthless person. Does that make sense to you?"

"It does. You're right. Okay, how does this sound: Mathematicians do it where it counts."

He threw back his head and laughed. I chuckled, pleased with myself.

"Come here," he said.

I did.

CHAPTER
10

I finished the article on Dilly and her students and sent it to Nancy. I spent the rest of the week mailing out queries, exercising, and trying, among other things, not to think about Jordan and me as a couple.

On Thursday and Friday mornings, I played racquetball with Tom Brant. We played hard, each of us wanting to demolish the other. We're both competitive types; we don't know how to be any other way.

I accepted this trait in Tom, but he couldn't quite see it as normal in me. That was because I wasn't a man. It didn't matter that he'd known his share of aggressive women, like the one who cut her boyfriend's face with a can opener. You know the kind of gadget. At one end, it has a sharp point for piercing. Then, after you get it through the lid, you saw away. According to Tom, she did.

It still didn't matter. I was a female and not supposed to want to vanquish him.

The second time we played, I did just that. I was lobbing balls against the front wall as hard as I could, and they were hitting the floor before Tom could take a swing at them. The final score was 21 to 5, favoring me. Tom said, "Are you sure you're not a lezzie?"

"I'm always impressed by how gracious you are in defeat," I said with a wide grin. "Not to mention your sensitivity toward discriminated-against minorities."

73

He shook sweat on me. "I could arrest you for impersonating a woman," he said.

"I could perform a citizen's arrest on you for impersonating a civilized human being," I said. "You're a sore loser."

"So?"

"Nothing. It was just a comment."

"Okay. I'll accept it if you treat me to coffee."

"Why not? But let's have it at my house. Come over after you get cleaned up, and I'll serve it to you with a chocolate doughnut."

What I really wanted to do was pump him for information about the Dilly Friedman case. He had to know more than I did, which was nothing.

We parted company. I changed into clean, dry clothes and headed for home. Tom showed up about ten minutes after I got there. We were standing in the hall, getting ready to go in the kitchen, when we heard a thump on my front door. I said, "What was that?"

Tom pushed me behind him before squinting through the peephole. "I don't see anything," he said, "but stay back. It could be a bomb."

"Then staying behind you won't really do it."

He ignored me. After staring through the peephole one more time, he cautiously opened the door. He glanced down, whistled, then took off running.

"What is it?" I said to his departing back. When I got no answer, I checked out the scene for myself. It took about a second to see it. It was on my front step. It was a rat, but not a wild rat. It was white, the kind of rodent you buy at a pet store to feed to your boa constrictor. It was dead.

Now, some people might say the best rat is a dead rat, but I doubt they would include this one. Even before I crouched down to get a better look, I could tell that its throat had been cut from ear to ear. A thin line of blood marked where the knife had traveled.

I was pretty sure the rat hadn't committed suicide on my step because I didn't see any knife. I also didn't think a neighbor's cat had brought it to me as a love offering. Someone had deliberately killed this rat and thrown it at my door. I took off running in the opposite direction from Tom.

It was a beautiful day, warm but breezy. If I'd had a more benign reason for running, I would have enjoyed myself instead of worrying.

I ran for about three blocks. I saw a dark-haired woman strolling slowly down the main street, a couple walking a big German shepherd, and about a million kids. I didn't know any of them and couldn't think of a reason why they'd want to harass me. Finally, I turned back.

Tom was already at my house when I got there. He was dripping with sweat again. This time he didn't try to put any on me. It was obvious he considered this serious business.

"Did you see anyone suspicious?" I asked, although the answer was apparent. He wouldn't have been standing around with if he had.

"No, just a pregnant woman pushing a stroller with two kids in it. I seriously doubt any of them did it. You know, this place makes me sick. There are so few fences and so much open land that a bad guy can take off and disappear just like that."

Tom looked at me accusingly. "Why do you think that thing is on your doorstep?"

"I put it there, of course, in case people want to wipe their feet off before coming in."

"Very funny." He bent over the rat. "Jesus Christ!"

I'm pretty wary about taking Jesus's name in vain because I'm Jewish and thus unsure about the whole

Christian religious etiquette thing. Nevertheless, when Tom said that, I said, "Ditto."

"Its throat has been cut."

"A kosher kill," I said.

He frowned at me. "What are you talking about?"

"You know. We've discussed it. Jews who keep kosher can only eat certain animals which have been killed in a prescribed way, by having the jugular vein severed. That's how this rat was done in, not that we eat rats."

Tom looked shocked. "Are you saying you think a Jew killed this rat?"

I started to laugh. "Are you saying you're taking me seriously?"

Tom flushed and glared at me. "Did I ever tell you I don't like you, Rachel?"

I laughed again, and he relaxed. "Look," I said, "there's a trash can at the curb. Would you mind putting the corpse in it?"

"I don't know. It might be evidence."

"I told you I was just kidding."

"No, I mean it."

"Evidence of what?"

He stared hard at me. "You tell me, Rachel."

I shook my head.

"Who have you offended lately, besides me?"

"Nobody. Well . . ."

"Well what?"

"I might have irritated a stray person here and there."

"Get inside," he said. "I'm going to dispose of this thing."

After he'd come back from the curb and, at my insistence, washed his hands, he seated himself across from me at the kitchen table. I poured him coffee and handed him a cake doughnut with chocolate icing. He stuffed half of it in his mouth before mumbling, "Talk!"

"There is one person who might be annoyed with me."

He swallowed and said clearly, "Does this have anything to do with the Dilly Friedman case?"

"How did you know that?" I asked.

"I know it because I know you. When you get hold of something, you don't let go until it's worked out to your satisfaction."

I smiled at him. "Thank you."

"I didn't mean it as a compliment. Okay, what's the possible connection with Friedman?"

I sat back in my chair and folded my hands in front of me, a stupid habit forced on me in elementary school that I've never been able to get rid of. "I guess you remember what I told you about the Six-Pack," I said.

"Vaguely."

"Hasn't anyone at the station mentioned them?"

He lifted his shoulders in a shrug. "Could have. As I said before, it's not my case. Besides, I've got plenty of my own to worry about."

"So you're not involved at all?"

He shifted his feet under the table. "I help out a little. We're understaffed at the moment."

"I knew it," I said triumphantly. "Tell me everything."

"There's not much to tell. We still don't know who killed her or why she was killed."

"I'm concentrating on the Six-Pack," I said. "I think you guys should, too."

Tom gave me a disapproving look. "You shouldn't be concentrating on anyone. It's not your business."

I made my face look innocent as I prepared to tell a lie. "Look," I said, "I'm still working on the article. I've been interviewing these guys, or trying to, to get information on Dilly when she was in school and studying special ed. I want to know if they saw any evidence of future promise in her." I frowned. "So far, I haven't gotten anywhere. I don't even know the name of one of them. Why don't you help me out? I know you could if you wanted to."

He seemed to struggle with himself for a while, then through tight lips repeated the names, including the one I hadn't heard before. "I knew you knew who they were," I said accusingly. "Who's that last guy?"

"You mean Brad Kramer? He works for one of the food companies here. I think he's in advertising or something. Very respectable, of course."

"Does he have an alibi for the day of Dilly's murder? Do any of them?"

He shrugged, a habitual gesture with him. "Nobody asked them. There wasn't any reason to. Maybe we will now. Tell me which of them you irritated."

"Okay. Actually, there might be two. One would be Jim Cohen."

"The political type?"

"Yes. I've called him several times, but he hasn't called back."

"So how did you irritate him?"

"I said I might have. Maybe he didn't like my calling him. He certainly isn't breaking his neck to get in touch with me."

"And the other one?"

"That would be Dicky Miller. He's the bus driver."

"Is that what he is? I heard his name, but that's all.

"Yes, he drives the little bus that goes around the villages. I questioned him recently about Dilly. He didn't seem too pleased that I did."

"Displeased enough to throw a rat at your door?"

"It's possible."

Tom went to the closet where I kept my phone books. He took down the one for Fairfield. "I'll give him a call," he said. "He might talk to me over the phone. If not, I'll ask one of the detectives on the case to pay him a visit."

He looked through the phone book, then threw it down in disgust. "Do you know how many Richard Millers live in Fairfield?"

I shook my head.

"Too many. I think I'll give the bus company a call. They'll give me his number."

He dialed, asked to speak to a supervisor, and explained what he wanted. After that, all I heard were a few grunts from Tom and some innocuous You-don't-say?-type things.

"What?" I said. "What's going on?"

Tom ignored me until after he hung up. "Dicky Miller doesn't drive a bus anymore. He quit last week. When did you talk to him?"

"Last week."

"Wonderful."

"I refuse to take the blame for him quitting. Where is he now?"

"They don't know. The person I spoke with said that Dicky's been with them a long time. He used to leave every once in a while to play in a band, but he never quit before. They didn't want him to go, said they'd hold the job for him. He said no; it was time to get out of here. What the hell did you say to him?"

"Nothing. I just asked him a few questions about his relationship with Dilly when they were at the university together. He said they were friends, but she was never his woman. That's all."

"It looks like something spooked him."

"Did you get his home phone number?"

"Yeah, and his address. I'll try calling him first."

Tom held the phone for a few moments, then banged

it down. "Disconnected," he said, sounding outraged. "Come on, let's drive over. He lives in an apartment building on the other side of Twenty-nine. Maybe he's still there."

It used to be that it was easy to get to the other side of Fairfield. Now the place has grown so much, and the traffic is so heavy at times, that we've got a number of cloverleafs that make getting around more complicated. At least that's true if you're not sure where you're going. But Tom knew every bit of the area.

The apartment complex was the typical kind of place Fairfield people who don't have lots of money live in. All the buildings were gray, with big windows to light the stairwells. Each unit contained a basement floor, with three apartments and a laundry room, then stairs that went up three floors. Dicky's building was the last one on the left. The number on his mailbox was 300.

We went up to the third floor and banged on his door. Nobody answered. Finally, Tom and I went to the apartment next to Dicky's. Although it was lunchtime already, the guy who came to the door looked as though he'd just gotten up.

"Yeah, I know Dicky," he said in reply to Tom's question. "He moved out."

"Do you know where he went?"

"I haven't a clue. He just said he wasn't going to hang around here anymore."

I said, "Suppose he had wanted to stay in the area for a few days. Was there anyone who would have taken him in?" I was thinking about the rat. I couldn't picture Miller commuting from Colorado or wherever to pitch something at my front door.

"Maybe. I don't know. Look, man, I have to go back to bed. I had a hard night." He smiled at Tom, winked at me, then shut his door.

After we were heading back to my house, I asked Tom, "What do you think?"

I got the shrug.

"He could have thrown the rat."

"Yeah, maybe. He could also have left the place. That's what he told his neighbor he was going to do."

"Maybe he's dead."

Tom frowned at me. "Why do you say that?"

"I don't know. Somebody killed Dilly. Maybe that person got rid of Dicky Miller, too."

"Yeah. And maybe that person tossed a rat at your door. And maybe that person is going to want to kill you, Rachel, unless you leave things alone. Try thinking about that."

CHAPTER
11

Cleome tilted her head to one side and fixed me with a hard brown stare. She said, "I bet I've seen more shootings and knifings than you."

"I'm jealous," I answered with what I thought was the right degree of sarcasm—just a tinge because she was a kid and I knew I shouldn't be fighting with her, but enough to let her know I wasn't swayed by her argument.

The two of us were disagreeing about whether Cleome should be involved in any way in the Dilly Friedman case. I'd told her about the rat incident shortly after I picked her up in Baltimore. Back inside my house, I was trying to get her to agree that the rat was meant to be a threat. She said she knew more about violence (thus the reference to shootings), not to mention rats, than I did. "And ours are big and mean," she said, "not puny little white ones like you got here."

"It doesn't matter. You're a child."

She put her hands on her hips. Unlike her small breasts, her hips hadn't rounded into maturity yet; they were still those of a sturdily built preteen. She said, "My pastor says, a little child shall lead you."

"He didn't mean you, Cleome."

"How do you know that? You ever been in my church?"

"No, but I know he was referring to a messiah, not a ten-year-old girl."

She said sulkily, "I liked Ms. Friedman better. She wouldn't hear about that, wouldn't argue with me, neither. She was Jewish."

"So am I."

She shook her head. "I thought Jewish people don't bother about Jesus. That's what Miss Friedman said." This last was announced as though Dilly had been the final word and the issue was settled for all time.

"Doesn't matter," I said, sounding as pigheaded as she did. "Besides, the line comes from Isaiah, which is in the Old Testament, the Jewish Bible. I've read it. A Jewish man wrote it—and he also wasn't referring to you."

"Is that right? I wonder if Pastor Gibbins knows that." I refrained from comment.

On this visit, Cleome was wearing a yellow T-shirt and a pair of bright green shorts. She would have looked nice except for the fact that the shirt had a hole in it and one of the shorts pockets was torn and hanging out like a thirsty dog's tongue. Her left blue sneaker looked as though it had been worked over by the same dog. I said, "Where did you get those clothes?"

She gave me a belligerent look. "Why?"

"I was just wondering."

"Lord and Trailer. Where'd you get yours?"

I was in my usual grungy outfit of blue sweatshirt and pants. The latter were hacked off at just above the knees in deference to the warm weather. I said, "Same place."

We both laughed then, and I hugged her. She stiffened slightly but didn't back off in a hurry. I said, "How about something to eat?"

"I could maybe eat a little. What do you have?"

This was my big moment. I put out tuna- and egg-salad sandwiches, with lettuce and sliced tomatoes, celery stuffed with pimento cheese, milk, and Danish pastries. Cleome sat down at the kitchen table, discarded the lettuce and tomatoes, ignored the celery, and ate everything else. "That's pretty good," she said when she'd finished. "Thank you."

She seemed innately polite. I had noticed that before. In fact, I'd noticed it about a lot of the children at the Nettie Blue School. It was a nice trait. I liked it.

"Now," she said, "where are we in Miss Friedman's case?"

I started to argue with her again about thinking she was involved in any way. Then I decided to drop it. I'd just see to it that talking about the murder was all we did. When I made more visits to get information, and I planned to, I wouldn't take her with me. She'd be all right.

I told her about Dicky Miller, about our conversation and his subsequent disappearance.

"Why you think he left?" she said.

Before I could tell her what I thought, she said, "Somebody knocking. You think it's the murderer?"

I didn't really, but I approached the door cautiously and peered out through the peephole. "It's my friend," I said.

I opened the door and in walked Nancy Martin. As usual, she looked gorgeous. It wasn't just her height and extreme slenderness, or even her fairy-princess pale gold hair and coolly beautiful face, that created the effect. Her green Ungaro pants suit (I knew who the designer was because she'd told me) was stunning and fit her perfectly.

"Nancy, this is Cleome Hightower," I said.

"Hello, Cleome." Nancy sounded gracious.

"Cleome, this is Ms. Martin."

Cleome didn't move, didn't speak.

"Cleome, hon, did you hear me?"

"Yes," she said in a dazed voice. "Hi."

She could hardly get the word out. She seemed thunderstruck or, more accurately perhaps, starstruck. She was looking at Nancy as though this year's Academy Award winner for best actress had just walked in and greeted her.

She stood. I waited for her to genuflect—or at least kiss Nancy's ring. Instead, she shuffled her feet, then bent the one that had the chewed-up shoe on it.

I sniffed. Cleome hadn't acted that way around me. She hadn't cared that I noticed her shoe.

Nancy gave her a queenly smile. "Sit down, dear," she said. She turned to me. "And where does she come from?"

"Baltimore," Cleome croaked before I could get a syllable out.

"What are you doing so far from home?"

"Visiting."

Nancy looked at me. "Cleome was a student of Dilly Friedman, the special education teacher I wrote about. She stays with me sometimes on the weekends."

"Is that so?"

"Yes, it's so."

"Since when?"

I shrugged.

I was irritated, but I didn't know why. Nancy was one of my dearest friends, yet all of a sudden, I didn't like her much.

Ignoring me, Nancy gave Cleome the once-over. The little girl smiled shyly and patted her hair. I was disgusted.

Nancy stood. "Let's go," she said.

I glared at her. "Go where?"

"To take Cleome shopping, of course. There's a Walcott's for Kids at the Mall."

"I was planning to take her shopping," I said, hoping I didn't sound as defensive as I felt. "I just hadn't gotten around to it yet."

Cleome said, "If you want to shop, there's a flea market real close to my house."

I said, "I was thinking of Kmart."

"Walcott's will be better," Nancy said. "Trust me."

It was obvious that Cleome did. She walked out with Nancy without a backward glance at me. I trailed reluctantly behind.

We drove to the Mall in Nancy's Lincoln. The parking lot appeared to be about full, but as usual, Nancy found a place, right next to one of the entrances, too. We went inside. The Mall was crowded with the usual eager Saturday shoppers. Not that many were going into Walcott's. When I looked at the prices on a few of the clothes, I could see why. This place was not for the peasants.

But, of course, Nancy wasn't a peasant. The saleswoman seemed to recognize that immediately and addressed all remarks to her as though I weren't there. Cleome was also treated like royalty; after all, look who she was with.

We finally finished about an hour later. The bill came to over six hundred dollars, which Nancy put on her American Express card. "Listen," I said, "I can't afford this kind of largesse. I can chip in a hundred, but that's it." I never tried to impress Nancy, so it wasn't hard for me to say this. Well, okay, it was a little bit hard, but that was because I wanted to be the one who bought stuff for Cleome.

"Save your money," she said. "This was fun. Did you have fun, Cleome?"

Up to that point, I would have been certain she'd have said yes. Now I wasn't so sure. Cleome was like a deflated balloon. "We've got to take everything back," she said. "I don't need them clothes."

Nancy said, "Of course you do."

"No, ma'am, I don't want them."

Maybe for the first time since I'd known her, Nancy lost her composure. "I picked them out for you," she said in the loudest voice I'd ever heard her use—which still made it lower than my everyday calm voice. "You're going to keep them."

Cleome shook her head.

"What is it, honey?" I said.

She came over to the other side of me, as far away from Nancy as she could get while still continuing to be with us, and whispered in my ear. "If I bring these home, somebody will steal them."

I don't know how I knew, but I did. Cleome didn't want to say it, but what she meant was that her mother, the crack addict, would sell the clothes for drugs; the slacks and shorts and tops, the jackets and dresses wouldn't stay in the kid's possession any time at all. I said, "How about leaving them at my place? Then when you visit on the weekends, you can wear them instead of having to bring stuff from home."

Nancy still seemed bewildered, but Cleome gave me a grateful look and squeezed my hand. Nancy might be the fairy godmother, but it was I who'd been designated the mother role. I suddenly felt much better. I remember I gave Nancy a pitying look.

After Nancy dropped us off, I spent the rest of the day feeding Cleome and watching her try on her new clothes. We had a good time.

The next morning didn't start off quite as well. First, Cleome couldn't decide what to wear. After we got that straightened out, she asked me to fix her hair.

"Me? I can't do that. It's too complicated, with all those parts and little braids and things."

"You're a nice white lady, Miss Rachel, but you don't got too much smarts."

I felt sort of hurt, though I knew I shouldn't have. My hair was naturally curly. All I ever did was keep it short, wash it, and run a brush through it when it was almost dry. I didn't defend myself, though. I said, "I'm sorry."

Cleome patted my hand. "Don't worry. I'll teach you. I taught Miss Friedman."

"Oh yeah?" I said, my competitive nature coming to the fore. "Well, if she could learn, I can, too."

"Right. Where's your bottle of Optimum Care?"

"I don't have any. I never heard of it."

"It's oil. You don't got none, I guess we have to go without it. Okay, first thing, you got to brush and comb my head."

"Can't you do that?"

She gave me a pitying look. "Never mind. We got the sections here already. We'll just leave them."

Thank goodness for that. I said, "Now what?"

"Put the knockers on."

I raised my eyebrows.

Cleome shook her head. "That ain't what you're thinking."

The knockers were pointed out to me. I put a white one on a section of hair, then braided it, finishing with a green barrette on the end. I went section by section.

When I finished, I was as proud of myself, and as exhausted, as if I'd climbed Mount Everest without any Sherpas.

After that we had breakfast. That's when Cleome brought up the subject of Dilly's murder again.

"You think the person who killed her knew her?"

I said I was starting to get that feeling after my conversation with Dicky Miller. "He must have some information," I said.

"He must have done it."

"Why do you say that?"

"Why would he run away if he didn't?"

"I don't know."

"He's afraid because he did it." She said this with utter conviction.

"It could have been something else."

She stared at me, her face solemn, dimples nowhere in evidence. "Yeah. Maybe he was killed, too, because he knew too much. Maybe he knew the one who did it."

I nodded. "That would mean two murders have been committed, and the killer is still in business."

"How are we going to put him out?" I shook my head. "You want me to find out if we can get somebody to hit him? I could ask around some of my mama's friends."

"I don't think we'll do that, at least not yet," I said. "Let's think about this some more. Suppose Dicky Miller did kill Miss Friedman. Why did he do it, and why did he do it now? Why didn't he do it years ago when he went to school with her?"

Cleome shook her head.

I said, "We need to look for a motive for him to have wanted to kill her."

"Yeah, and we got to do it before he kills us. You think he's planning to do that?"

I said no. I hoped she believed me. I wished I did. Somebody out there was ruthless, and neither I nor the police had a clue as to who it was.

CHAPTER
12

It was Monday. Cleome was back in Baltimore and, I hoped, in school. I needed to work on more queries, but I knew I was kidding myself.

I wanted to talk to Jim Cohen about Dilly, if for no other reason than that he didn't want to talk to me. I considered storming his office but gave up on the idea. I doubted I'd get past the receptionist. There had to be a better way.

The phone rang. It was Nancy. Of course. I should have thought of it before. Nancy could get me in to see Cohen. She was a power in this area. "Jim Cohen doesn't want to talk to me," I said.

"Who does? I dialed you, and even I don't want to talk to you."

"Very funny. He doesn't return my calls."

"Why do you want to talk to him?"

"I need to ask him what his involvement with Dilly Friedman really was and whether he killed her."

"I can't see any reason why he'd object to those subjects."

"So how are you going to get me in?"

There was silence. I waited.

"I'll tell him that I'm sending someone over to interview him for the magazine. He'll be thrilled."

"Not when he sees me," I said.

"That's true, but he won't dare turn you away. You might say uncomplimentary things about him, and then I might do the same."

"Will you really publish an article on him?"

"Why not? I'll call him; then I'll call you back."

In about five minutes, she did. "He's waiting for you. That is, he's waiting for a representative from the *Target*. You won't have any trouble being admitted."

"Unless he sees me first. Thanks, pal. Good-bye."

"Wait. The reason I called you originally was to ask you something."

I had an idea of the subject. All I said, though, was, "Oh?"

"How's that little girl . . . Cleome, isn't it?"

As though she didn't remember. I knew her better. "Fine," I said casually. "I drove her home yesterday."

"Did she take any of her new clothes?"

"Certainly not. They'd just be sold. I know about those things, Nancy. You don't."

For the first time ever, I heard her sputter, at a loss for words. I loved it. "I need to go," I said before she could get a coherent sentence out, and hung up. That would teach her to play Lady Bountiful to my protégée, I thought, at the same time knowing it wouldn't teach her anything.

I changed into one of my few nice dresses, a pale blue linen with a half belt in back. It made me look taller—not that I ever think of myself as short, in spite of what some people say. Then I stepped outside.

There was a brown-haired doll, wearing a pink frilly dress and cute little white shoes, lying facedown on my top step. At first, I thought it had been left there by some neighborhood kid. I turned it over and started to pick it up, hoping I could identify and return it to its owner. Then I got a good look at it and changed my mind. This wasn't some little girl's plaything that had been thrown on my step and forgotten. Someone had gone to a lot of trouble with this doll, someone who had meant it just for me.

How did I know that? It was easy. A blown-up picture of my face had been pasted over the doll's so that none of its features were visible. Only mine. The picture of me was recent, obviously taken when I had been standing on my front steps.

That was weird enough, but it was the rest of the doll that got to me. In the place where its heart would have been if it had been alive, someone had stuck three tailor's pins; one had obviously been pushed in so hard it was bent. Red ink, drawn to look like blood, had been sketched on the dress, starting at the pinholes and going down to the hem. Because of the type of material the dress was made of, some gauzy stuff I couldn't identify, it had soaked up the ink. What I imagined had been meant to suggest a stream of blood had been absorbed by the fabric and, instead of a stream, was a series of blotches. They looked remarkably like bloodstains to me.

I'd been killed, symbolically. Why this, and why had someone tried to freak me out with a dead rat outside my door? Whose skin was I getting under?

I had the questions; I wished I had the answers. Maybe Jim Cohen could help. I got in my car, threw the doll in the backseat, and headed for his office.

When he wasn't running for County Council, Jim Cohen was a lawyer. His legal office was downtown, in a large new building near the main mall and next to an armed forces recruiting center. The lobby was floored in white marble punctuated by tubs filled with palm trees. There was a guard right inside the doors. I had to sign in.

The elevator I took to the eleventh floor was quiet and nearly empty. I stepped out onto a carpet covering a long hallway. Glass doors bore the names of the businesses inside. Jim's said COHEN, MCCARTHY, AND COHEN, ATTORNEYS-AT-LAW.

The hallway hadn't had any odor but that of newness. Jim's outer office, however, smelled like diluted aftershave. I wondered if it was meant to suggest masculinity held loosely in check. The music being piped in was nondescript, designed neither to delight nor to offend.

Jim was standing by the receptionist's desk. From his smile, he was apparently expecting someone, but not me. The smile quickly faded and he put his hand to his mouth. I wondered what he was trying to conceal. Was it guilt at having left a voodoo doll outside my door?

"Hi," he said unenthusiastically. "I guess you came to see me. I wish I could talk to you, but I'm afraid I have an appointment."

"With a reporter from the *Howard County Target*?"

His shoulders slumped. "Are you it?"

"I'm it."

"Okay. Come on in." His voice was filled with resignation.

He was as good-looking as I remembered: tall and slim, with blond hair, blue eyes, and nice, if undistinguished, features. He was wearing a dark blue suit, white shirt, and red power tie. His black shoes were highly polished, and he wore black socks. I was certain the socks went up over his calves because anything shorter would have been gauche, and James Cohen was definitely not gauche. He was smooth.

His office was standard attorney-on-the-way-up. There was an appropriately worn Oriental rug on the floor, a handsome brown leather chesterfield and two leather chairs, and a large mahogany desk with a piece of glass on top to protect its surface. The glass held a picture in a brown leather frame of a young woman as blond as Jim

Cohen, a paperweight with a Japanese scene painted on it, and several brown leather boxes filled with paper clips and severely sharpened pencils. On the wall behind the desk were a number of framed diplomas and awards. Cohen sat at the desk and pointed me to a chair.

I noticed he wasn't wearing a wedding ring. I picked up the picture. "Your sister?"

He flashed me a charming grin. "My wife. Other people have remarked on the similarity in our looks."

The grin disappeared. "I don't have a lot of time, Ms. Crowne. Are you going to interview me about my political beliefs or poor Dilly Friedman?"

"How about both?"

He sat back in his chair. I got the disarming smile again. "All right. If that's what you want. Let's talk about politics here in Howard County first, Rachel. You don't mind if I call you Rachel, do you?"

"Not at all, but let's talk about you and Dilly first."

Jim Cohen pushed his chair upright and away from the desk. He stood. "Look. I don't mean to be rude, but I wish you wouldn't say that. There isn't any me and Dilly. I and four other guys were friends with her in school. We graduated. The guys and I didn't see each other much after that. I didn't see Dilly at all. The friendship among us is no longer important. That's it."

"Why didn't you see each other? Did anything happen?"

He sat down again. I sensed he liked having that large piece of furniture between us. "Sure. Life happened. We went our separate ways. One of us even became a bus driver."

"Dicky Miller," I said.

For a moment, I thought Jim looked frightened. "Where did you get that name?"

"Mrs. Pearl told me about him. Also, I went to speak to him."

"Dear Mrs. Pearl," he said bitterly. "Trying to prove she's not a snob by being everybody's friend and helper."

"Is she a snob?"

"Of course. She always thought Everett was better than the rest of us. He was the new Picasso."

"Leonardo da Vinci," I said.

"Whatever."

"Was he talented?"

Jim squirmed in his seat. "I don't know. Maybe. Painting isn't my field. Look, let's talk about how things are run in the county, shall we?"

I said, "Not just yet."

I thought he would act angry, but he didn't. He got up again, this time to sit on the end of the desk nearest me. His knees almost touched mine. "All right, you win. Dilly and I were friends with Ev Pearl, Dicky Miller, Bob McCauley, and Brad Kramer."

"Yeah?"

"Truthfully, we were always different from each other. We had different aspirations. For example, McCauley wanted to be a minister."

"And he is, right?"

"Why ask me if you already know?"

"How about Kramer?"

Jim laughed. "He wanted to be rich."

"Did he get his wish?"

"He will. He's marrying the daughter of the president of the company where he works. I saw the announcement a few months back in the *Washington Post*. He'd have a lot to lose if there was any negative talk about him."

I said, "Why should there be?"

Cohen looked uncomfortable. "I can't imagine."

"Then why did you say it?"

He frowned at me. "It was a general statement, that's all. I didn't mean anything special by it."

Like hell he didn't. I wanted to push him on it, but I had a feeling I'd be out of there really fast if I did. Because it had been so difficult getting to see him in the first place, I decided not to take the chance. I said, "How did you all get along together in school? Any problems?"

"None."

"Was Dilly closer to one of you than the others?"

I expected him to say she was closest to Everett Pearl, hands down. After all, they were engaged, or about to be. But he didn't. "I don't know. Maybe. If she was, it was probably to Everett. She said he was more sensitive than the rest of us." He gave me a comradely grin. "If it was sensitivity she was looking for, why didn't she hang out with girls?"

I assumed the question was rhetorical, as well as being implicitly sexist, and ignored it. "What did she mean by 'sensitive'?"

"I haven't a clue. It was her word, not mine. Anyway, we had fun for a while, but it wasn't the sort of friendship that could last outside the school setting. After graduation, when we went into different areas of study and work, there wasn't anything to keep us together. The usual story."

He stopped talking. I waited. "Oh, and, of course, Everett died."

"Tell me about that," I said.

"Why?"

"Okay. Don't tell me. Tell me more about Dilly."

He sighed and turned his hands outward. They were slender, the fingers long. "She was good-natured. She was a bit dizzy. She liked kids and wanted about a dozen of her own."

"Yet she didn't have any."

"Maybe nobody wanted to make them with her."

I looked up from my notes.

"I'm sorry. That's a pretty flippant way to talk about the dead, isn't it?"

I shrugged. "It doesn't matter. I'm sure she doesn't care. Not now."

He slid away from me and stood. "Are you really as tough as you sound?"

Was I? "I'll have to think about that," I said, brushing it off. "Tell me, do you have any ideas as to why she might have been killed?"

This time the fright was obvious. "How should I know? Are you suggesting . . . ?"

"Nothing, Mr. Cohen. I'm just searching."

"Why?"

"I'm interested in doing an article on violence here in Eden," I said off the top of my head. "You know, this doesn't seem like a place where bad things would occur."

"Well, you're wrong."

"Oh?"

"Do you know how much the current county council wastes every year on stupid schemes? Do you know how crazy some of these schemes are? Even an idiot shouldn't be tempted to try them. However, if I'm elected, all that will change."

I let him go on. I figured he'd earned it. And go on he did—for fifteen more minutes, at least, with hardly a pause for breath. It probably would have been longer, but I made him stop by standing up.

"Going already?" said the guy who couldn't wait to get rid of me a short time before.

"I have things to do. Unless you have more to tell me about you and Dilly."

"Of course I don't," he snapped. "I have more to tell

you about you and me, though. It's not just Brad Kramer who's concerned about scandal. If there were even a hint of it attached to my name, the damage to my career, and not just as an attorney, would be irreparable. My opponent would win. That's not fair, Rachel, and that's not right. I deserve to win."

"I didn't say you didn't."

"No, but if you're going to dig around and stir up old events . . ." He didn't finish the sentence.

"Such as what?"

"Such as nothing," he said angrily. "Don't be absurd. What could possibly have happened?"

"I don't know, Jim, but I think something did, and I mean to find out. If not me, the police."

His even teeth bit into his lower lip. "Is that a threat? It isn't a good idea to make threats."

"Of course not. I don't do that."

He stared at me a moment, then said, "I get it. You're looking for money, aren't you?"

Boy, was that a leap. What was going on here? "Why would you want to give me money?"

"I wouldn't, and I won't, but you sound like a blackmailer."

"I'm not, but I'd like to know what you think I could blackmail you about."

"Everybody has something."

"What's yours?"

He looked at me with distaste. "You're unrelenting, aren't you?"

"They don't call me Pit Bull for nothing."

"You know, Rachel, this could be a dangerous thing you're meddling in. Dilly was murdered. You could be, too. Maybe that's something you should think about."

"Is that what the rat and doll were for, to make me think?"

If he was an actor, he was a good one. He looked at me as though I wasn't even speaking English. "What did you say?"

"Should I think about danger in relation to you?"

His fists clenched. "I didn't kill Dilly. The thought is absurd and repugnant to me. But someone did, and that person isn't going to want you fishing around. If a man has killed once, I imagine it would be easier—and more necessary—to do it again. Maybe you should worry about that."

I've always been moved by logic, not to mention dead rats and dead dolls that look like me. I had to admit reason was on his side.

CHAPTER
13

I still hadn't gotten over the bleeding doll incident. When the bell rang the morning after I saw Jim Cohen, I peered cautiously through the peephole. I wondered what it might be this time—two rats and two dolls, or worse? Threats had to escalate, didn't they, or they'd be ineffective.

What I saw wasn't a threat at all, at least not to my physical being. It was Jordan Goldman, holding a bouquet of pink roses and baby's breath and wearing a self-satisfied smile.

I flung open the door and pulled him into the house. He was dressed in a short-sleeved pale yellow shirt and dark blue slacks. The shirt was open a little at the neck. I thought he looked gorgeous.

Apparently, he construed my haste in hauling him inside as sexual hunger. His smile grew broader. "Impatient devil, aren't you?"

A closer examination of my face must have changed his mind. "Something's wrong, Rachel. What is it?"

I had no intention of telling him about the rat or the doll because I knew how he'd react: he'd think I was stupid for meddling and get angry with me. That's the way he was.

I said, "I'm in shock, of course. You brought me flowers. You have to admit, that's not an everyday event."

He gave me a suspicious look. "I don't think . . ."

I grabbed him around the waist, the easiest place to get hold of because he was so much taller than I, and hugged him. "It's true," I said. "I'm thrilled."

I could tell his doubt lingered—this was no dope, after all—but he let himself be sidetracked by my enthusiasm. "Aren't they beautiful," I said, taking them from him. "What's the occasion?"

"Does there have to be one?"

"No, of course not." As I headed into the kitchen with the flowers, I said, "We need to find a vase for these. Then you'll have to tell me where I should put them."

He grinned. "Why not in the bedroom? You can look at them after I make love to you, and feel good about the flowers all over again."

"And then?"

"Then you can make love to me, to show your continued appreciation."

Didn't I know he was a smart guy!

I filled a container with water, poured in some of that stuff that's supposed to keep flowers alive practically forever but never works for me, and added the bouquet. Jordan stood behind me, hands on my shoulders. I felt a gentle propulsion, and he began to steer me in the direction of my bedroom. I grabbed the vase and let myself be maneuvered.

"Damn," I said when the doorbell rang.

"Don't answer it."

"I have to. I won't be able to concentrate otherwise."

He let go of me. I set the flowers on a table and walked to the door. "Who is it?" I yelled.

"It's me, Rachel. Let me in."

It was Tom, whom I did not want to invite into the house. I was afraid that besides breaking the romantic mood, he'd blab to Jordan about the rat. Fortunately, I hadn't told him about the doll incident, or I would have worried that he'd tell Jordan about that, too.

"I have company," I said through the door. "I'll call you later."

"Who's the company?"

I wasn't going to get rid of him. With a sigh, I opened the door. "Oh, it's you," he said looking past me to Jordan.

Tom didn't dislike him the way he did Nancy. He just didn't like him. If I thought about it, and I was doing that now, he didn't seem overly fond of anyone I cared about except maybe my brothers. I'd have to challenge him with that, but not just then.

My friend was wearing a red polo shirt that didn't quite cover his pot, khaki pants, and brown bedroom slippers. "Glad to see you," I said. "Why don't you go home?"

"What's the hurry?"

"Oh, you know. Jordan and I haven't been alone together for a while." I gave him a suggestive leer, hoping Jordan wouldn't notice it. "We have a lot to say to each other."

Tom plopped on my sofa. "Oh yeah?"

Stone brain! Sometimes I wished I'd never moved next door to him.

He gave Jordan an appraising look. "Did Rachel tell you about the rat?"

"What rat?" Jordan said, answering Tom's question. He drew up a chair so that he faced Tom. "Tell me."

I felt excluded. I'm sure they meant me to: two sane, sober guys discussing the crazy woman each was fond of in his way. I resented it. I said, "Why don't you both get out of here? I'm busy."

They ignored me as Tom described to Jordan the business with the rodent.

When my cop friend was finished, Jordan turned to me. He said, "Why do you do this sort of thing, Rachel? By no stretch of the imagination is it a normal activity for a writer."

If I'd ever intended to mention the doll, that convinced me that I mustn't. I'd go to my grave with the knowledge of it left unshared.

Instead, I said, "Why do you spend most of your life working on math problems that drive you nuts?"

"At least they don't throw rats at me."

He had a point, but it was one I chose not to respond to—mainly because I couldn't. I shrugged and said glibly, "We don't pick our problems."

This was baloney. I knew it, and he knew I knew it. Predictably he said, "The hell we don't. So what is it in you that makes you want to find out who committed a crime, no matter what?"

I could have come up with several reasonable answers, such as I don't like loose ends or I couldn't pass up a challenge; they might even have been accurate. But the real truth was that I didn't know. It was me; that's all.

"I can't help it," I said, "and I don't think I'm going to change."

He looked at me sadly. "I know you aren't."

He didn't say any more about it after that, but I got what he meant. He was wondering if a person like me was fit to be the mother of his two kids. Would I lead them into danger? Would I leave them and head off into danger myself?

I couldn't tell what conclusion he was going to come to, though I wasn't very hopeful. I also didn't know if I could behave differently even if I made the effort. Of course, I didn't expect to spend my life solving murders. If nothing else, the possibilities for getting involved in any more murder investigations were small. Still, I did intend to keep on writing and probing into things. I'd realized that I liked that. I also was aware that I could offend a lot of people. Some of them might prove to be a risk to my health.

"I brought her flowers," he said to Tom. The way he sounded made me feel that I'd died and he was burying me.

Tom said, "That's nice. Listen. The only way to stop her is to finish this case; then there won't be anything for her to do. Rachel says you're a problem solver. So, what do you think?"

At least Jordan was no longer looking disapprovingly at me. He wasn't looking at me at all. His attention was on Tom. "Tell me everything," he said.

Tom filled him in on what he knew about Dilly, how she'd died, people who had become suspects because they knew or had known her, and their alibis. Jordan listened patiently, then said, "But why would any of these people want to kill her?"

Tom sat back and crossed his legs. His brow wrinkled. "We aren't sure."

So smug, leaving me out of this. I said in a cranky voice, "I am."

That got their attention. "The killer is one of the Pack," I said. "He killed Dilly because she knew something about him that he didn't want to get out."

Tom said, "What did she know?"

I shrugged.

"When did this thing happen that she learned about?"

I shrugged again.

"Do you think it occurred recently? How do you know it didn't happen years ago?"

I said, "I think it did, probably five years ago, just before or after they all graduated. That makes sense; as far as I can tell, she didn't have much to do with any of them after that."

Jordan sat there, listening. Tom said, "So what was it?"

"I think you already asked me that. I don't know, but I can imagine possibilities."

"Like?"

"Like one or more of them broke the law in some way."

Tom gnawed at his lower lip. No doubt this was an expression of deep concentration, though not one I'd seen him use before. "Okay," he said. "What law was broken?"

"How about she saw one of them steal or vandalize something?"

Jordan said, "But wouldn't the police have been called in at the time?"

Tom shook his head. "Not necessarily. Besides, it could have been something else."

Jordan said, "Of course it could. It could have been lots of things. What's the worst one you can come up with?"

"A rape?" I said.

"We already checked," Tom shot back. "There was no report of a rape that might have involved her."

I thought some more. "A hit-and-run."

"That's a good one," he said, starting to get up from his seat. Then he changed his mind and slumped back down. "But why did the bad guy wait until now to off her?"

I didn't answer.

This time, Tom lifted his bulk off the couch. He moved closer until he was almost leaning over me. I felt he was trying to intimidate me, and doing a good job. I didn't like it. He said, "You don't know anything, Rachel."

I gave him a shove. "Back off, Brant."

He ignored me.

Jordan said, "I think she's generally right about what she believes, Tom. Dilly had information that could be harmful to one, maybe more than one, of the Pack. It was so bad that it affected her, made her become withdrawn. Still, because she was a nice girl, she never repeated it."

Tom said, "Then why kill her?"

Jordan stood up, too. He used his shoulder to thrust Tom out of the way. I could practically smell the testosterone, but both men acted as though nothing was going on. "There was always a chance she'd tell," Jordan said. "Only the person didn't worry about it as much before. Maybe he relaxed when nothing happened right away."

I could see that. "But then later . . . ?"

"Later—now—he had everything to lose. Dilly had become a real threat."

I said, "So he killed her."

Both of the guys said, "Right," like I needed them to approve my theory. I got up, too.

"However," Jordan said, "let's not get carried away with our brilliance. We're just guessing. We don't know that any of this stuff occurred. It's strictly conjectural."

"It's a hypothesis," I said, "and it's a good one. I think we should forget about anything that doesn't have to do with it and concentrate on that."

Tom patted his belly. He looked pleased. I didn't like it. He said, "It's what the detectives on the case think, that something happened back then that needs to be covered up now. That's the angle they're working."

"So why ask us all those questions?" I said, annoyed.

"Why not? It didn't hurt anything."

I said, "I'm going to hurt *you* if you don't leave. You've wasted enough of my time. Jordan's, too."

Tom had the gall to look insulted. "All right, if that's the way you feel. Will you be home later?"

"Not to you," I said.

He shook his head at Jordan as though to ask him how he put up with such an unreasonable individual. I let him show himself out.

When he was gone, I pushed Jordan into a chair and sat on his lap. I said, "Forget about Godzilla. Kiss me."

He looked at me glumly. "I'm not sure I feel like doing that, Rachel."

"Yes, you do." I put my arms around his neck. He stiffened. I pressed my lips against his. They were stiff, too. He was resisting me.

After a moment or two, he warmed toward me a little, but only a little. "Let's take the flowers into the bedroom," I said, at the same time getting up and pulling him to his feet.

We ended up on the bed, where I lovingly undressed him. It wasn't long before any misgivings he'd had evaporated. I could have told him *I'd* murdered Dilly, and he would have said that was swell.

Later, though, when we were in the kitchen, I saw him eyeing me uneasily. I could tell his doubts about me had come back. And what could I do about that? He had to work. I had to work. I couldn't keep him in my bed forever.

What verbal threats, rats, and spooky dolls couldn't do to me, his disaffection did. I'll admit it—I felt scared. This was a man I didn't want to lose. Still, I might have to. I had my pride. I hoped it wasn't all I was going to have.

CHAPTER
14

I hadn't seen or heard from Etta Pearl, Everett's mother, since I'd bumped into her at the Mall, so I was kind of surprised when she called me. She said she'd been thinking about me and wondered if I'd like to meet her for dinner.

I can't say I especially wanted to. I didn't figure we had too much in common. On the other hand, it wouldn't hurt me to do it. Maybe she'd even come up with some information I could use in tracking down the rest of Dilly's buddies. I said okay.

We agreed to eat at the King's Mistress restaurant. It was one of my favorite places, even though I only went there once or twice a year. That's because I couldn't afford to go more often. I wore my pale blue dress again.

The King's Mistress is Fairfield's most elegant restaurant. It's set in one of the newer villages, but it was there long before the village was. It had once been a private estate, and although there wasn't much land left around it anymore, it still had that estate look: a long, tree-lined drive ending in a beautiful four-story mansion, all lit up.

I had asked Etta if she wanted me to pick her up, but she'd said no. Although the restaurant has valet parking, I didn't see the attendant, so I left my Toyota down the drive and walked back to the entrance. I checked in with the maître d', a tall young guy with a haughty manner.

His style probably would have awed me when I was younger, but only amused me now. When I found that Etta hadn't gotten there yet, I went outside again to wait for her.

It was a nice night. Though there was only a slice of moon, the stars were bright and the sky clear. I liked the country quiet, too: noisy with the sounds of insects and birds but not with those of people.

I wasn't aware that Etta had arrived until she called out from her van and waved gaily to me. She parked in a handicapped space right in front of the restaurant while I waited on the sidewalk wondering what I could do to help or if I should even offer. I noticed that her van was equipped with hand controls.

She managed it all herself. The next thing, she was in her chair, on the sidewalk, her blanket spread over her lap and down to her navy blue shoes. Her dress was blue, too, with buttons the size and color of buttercups. She waited for me to accompany her up the ramp beside the steps.

"I don't come here often," she said with a smile as thrilled as that of a little girl offered a new doll, "but I do love this place. Look at the wide doorways and the deep windowsills. There's nothing skimpy here. I had to have all the doorways in my house made bigger five years ago when I became confined to this chair."

Everett had died five years before, right after he and Dilly had graduated. I'm sure the curiosity I felt about a possible connection showed in my eyes, but she didn't offer any more, and I couldn't bring myself to push the subject. I was bold, but I wasn't brazen.

Our conversation ended with the appearance of the maître d'. He led us to a large dining room, one of several. This one was painted, or daubed from the looks of it, a deep red. It was called, appropriately, the Red Dining Room. I liked it.

Etta and I settled in, and we studied the menu. I'm an omnivore and will eat anything but baby animals, which, of course, leaves out veal and lamb. Etta said she'd have what I was having, so I ordered barbecued duck for two, with garlic mashed potatoes and baby string beans. When it comes to vegetables, I show no mercy.

The food was excellent, and for a while our chatter was superficial while we concentrated on our meal. It wasn't until we were finishing that I brought up the subject of Dilly. "I'm still wondering about why she was killed," I said. "Nothing makes any sense so far. Can you think of a reason someone might have murdered her?"

She put down her fork and sat back. "Not one. As I said so many times before, she was a sweet girl. Only a madman would have done that to her."

"Maybe. But if he was, he wasn't an impulsive one."

She looked intrigued. "Really? Why do you say that?"

"This guy came prepared. Nothing seems to be missing from the house, so he must have brought along the weapon he hit her with as well as the rope. And he probably wore gloves, because there aren't any fingerprints there that shouldn't be."

"Is that what you learned from the police?"

I shot her a glance. "Why would you think the police would tell me anything?"

"Well, I know you live next door to a policeman."

I must have looked at her funny because she said, "Oh, dear, did I say something wrong?"

"Not wrong. Just curious. How do you know who lives next door to me?"

She stared into space for a second or two, then said, "I think Jim Cohen told me. Yes, that's who it was. Does that matter?"

I wondered how Cohen had found out, and why. I also wondered what reason he had for passing the information on to Etta Pearl. I thought of asking her, but decided to let it drop.

The waiter came by then with the dessert cart and gave us a little speech about each of the items on it. I was tempted but passed. I was watching my figure because I wanted Jordan to keep watching it, too.

Mrs. Pearl also didn't order dessert. "In my condition," she said, sounding apologetic, "I can't let myself gain too much." There was a pause. She said, "Are you listening to me, dear?"

Actually, I wasn't. I was looking at an attractive man of about sixty who was standing in the doorway of our room, studying Etta intently. This guy was tall and lean, with white hair and bright blue eyes. He was dressed in a well-tailored dark blue suit and white shirt that looked custom fitted and expensive.

I said, "Mrs. Pearl, do you know that man? I think he's staring at you."

She turned her head, then flushed when she caught sight of him. I could see the red run up from her neck. "He's my doctor," she said in a voice that suggested she wasn't any fan of his. "At least, he was. I don't go to him anymore. Oh my, he's coming over."

When he reached our table, he bent down and grasped Etta's hands. His were well-tended, the nails short and polished. I noticed that her fingers fluttered nervously in his hold. "Etta, how are you?" he said.

She looked up, but not quite into his eyes. "I'm doing fine. How are you?"

He said, "All right. I haven't seen you for—what is it, a year?"

She nodded stiffly. I guess it was embarrassing to dump your doctor and not tell him.

He inclined his head in my direction, said, "Do you mind?" and pulled up a chair next to her wheelchair.

"You look well," he said, adding in a lower voice, "Now, how are you really doing?"

For a moment I thought she was going to say something insulting to him, but all she said was, "This isn't the place for it, Doctor."

"You're right." He glanced my way apologetically. "How about making an appointment soon to talk."

I could tell from her expression even before she declined that she wasn't going to do it. She said, "You're a nice person, Dr. Pumphrey, and an excellent physician, I'm sure. But I decided there was no reason to keep on seeing you. I am as helpless now as I was on day one."

"That's not my fault, Etta." He sounded defensive.

She sighed. "I suppose not. I'm afraid that isn't the point, though. If I won't get better, why should I see a physician at all?"

He appeared shocked. "Do you mean to tell me that you aren't going to any doctor?"

She didn't answer.

"Mrs. Pearl, Etta, you can't do this to yourself. Wheelchair-bound people need to stay in touch with a health care provider. There can be kidney problems. There can be . . ." He stopped and glanced at me again. "I suppose this isn't dinner table conversation, is it? But can't you see, miss, that she mustn't ignore her condition?"

I agreed with him, of course. But since I didn't want to get into the discussion, I kept my mouth shut.

He turned back to Etta. "You still have your appointments with Dr. Burns, don't you?"

"The psychiatrist? Oh no. He wasn't any help. No matter what you prescribed, or what he said, I'm still paralyzed."

The doctor shook his head. "Then you're really not being seen by anyone."

"That's right."

"I'm sorry. You must feel that the medical profession has failed you."

"When I dance at your daughter's wedding, I'll say you didn't," she told him with a flirtatious smile. "How is your daughter?"

He frowned. "She ran off with a bantam-weight prizefighter."

Etta pushed her chair back. "It was nice seeing you again. Give my regards to your nurse. Good-bye, Dr. Pumphrey."

This time he flushed. I suspected he wasn't used to being dismissed. He rose and said, "I'll leave you ladies now. Forgive me for interrupting your dinner. I'd like you to call me, though, Mrs. Pearl."

"Certainly," she said in a way that let him know she never would.

After he left, she became visibly upset. Before I could say anything, she said, "Oh, Rachel, you don't know what it's like to be in my condition. The helplessness. The anguish. I'm not that old, you know."

What could I say? I *didn't* know what it was like to be paralyzed from the waist down. From what I could imagine, though, I believe I would have preferred to be dead. It wouldn't have been bearable for someone like me not to be able to get around. "I'm sorry," I said, echoing the good doctor.

With a discreet swipe of a tissue, she removed a tear. "It's not your fault. But never mind me. Never mind the doctor. I have something to tell you."

I was glad to have the subject changed. "What's that?" I said, hoping my relief didn't show.

"Do you remember when you asked me who all the members of Everett's group were and I couldn't remember some of the names? I know you wanted to talk to them, so I looked in Everett's yearbook and got their names for you. I have their work numbers, too."

That was a help. I said, "That was nice of you, Etta."

She gave me a smile that managed to seem modest and self-congratulatory at the same time. "No, not really. I want you to assist the police in finding Dilly's murderer. He mustn't get away with what he did. If you speak to those boys, maybe it will do some good. Anyway, I explained to them what you were after. I must say, Brad Kramer wasn't happy about your involvement."

"Why was that?"

"I don't know. It wasn't as though he hadn't heard of you. He said he thought you'd given up the idea of writing about Dilly."

Interesting. "I wonder who told him about me."

She shrugged. "Maybe it was Jim Cohen."

Cohen again? I said, "I didn't realize they kept in touch. In fact, I had the impression they didn't."

"Is that what Jim led you to believe? I'm sure they do. On a very informal basis, of course. Just as I keep in touch by calling them occasionally. I was always interested in Everett's friends. Besides, I wanted to congratulate Brad on his engagement. I'd seen the announcement in the *Post*. You know, it's not every day that an ordinary boy gets his big wish. What I mean is, he's going to marry the daughter of the president of the company where he works. Dilly told me he always meant to marry money."

There was more than a hint of maliciousness in her tone. Well, why not? Anyone who thinks suffering always ennobles people isn't paying attention.

I said, "It's uplifting to hear about someone who worked hard and achieved his goals."

I think at first she believed I was sincere. Then she

grinned and said, "Naughty girl." Nobody had called me that since before puberty.

I felt relieved when the waiter came over with the check. I needed to go home and finish an article I was working on. While I was thinking about that, Etta grabbed the check.

I didn't want her to pay for me. It would make me feel beholden to her; that's the way I am. I said, "Let's just split the bill. We both got the same thing."

Her expression grew stubborn. "It's my treat, dear."

I said no, but she held on to the check. What choice did I have? I couldn't wrestle with her. I gave in as graciously as I could.

I watched while she got into her van via a lift I hadn't noticed before. Then she folded her chair, stuck it in back of her seat, and waved good-bye. I might not have had a lot in common with her, but that didn't stop me from admiring her that night. I had a feeling that under the veneer of pre–women's lib helplessness there hid a gutsy, independent female.

I drove home, thinking mostly about meeting the remaining members of the Six-Pack. Maybe they'd have some idea why Dilly had changed after graduation.

I turned onto my street, parked in my drive, then walked up to the house. The visibility wasn't good, but since I was close to my front door, I didn't worry about my safety. As I recall, I was humming a tune I'd just heard on the radio, about love being like a knife.

I reached the top step and stopped. Something sticky touched my face. I figured it was a spider's web; I'd been attacked by their silky strands in just about that spot before. I backed off, wiped my hand across my face, then stretched out my arm to demolish the web so that I wouldn't walk into it again.

I hit something, but it wasn't as loose and airy as a

web. For a moment, I thought it was the spider and almost fell off the step. Then I realized it couldn't be, not unless the creature was wearing a little dress and had shoes on two of its eight feet. I wondered if I'd been left another doll with pins stuck in its heart.

I hadn't, although I was right about the doll part. This one had a blown-up picture of my face pasted over its face, like the last one. The difference was that this doll had a piece of plastic over its head and a rope around its small neck.

I pulled it down and took it into the house. That's where I discovered the worst of what it offered. Toward the back of the head, someone had poured a blob of red ink. It matted down the hair, making it look as though the doll's curls covered a bleeding, dangerous wound. Dilly's hair must have looked like that after she was struck.

I stared at the doll for several minutes. Thoughts swirled in my head, finally coming together in one thought: somebody out there—I could only assume it was Dilly's murderer—was not so subtly telling me to stop investigating her death.

That meant I had to be doing something right. I felt a rush of satisfaction.

CHAPTER
15

I was lying in bed the next morning, thinking about whether I was going to tell Tom what had happened the night before. I didn't want to, and not just because I was concerned that he'd tell Jordan. It was Tom's reaction I mainly wanted to avoid. He'd veer from anger, because I'd maybe been in jeopardy, to disbelief, because I couldn't actually prove that someone had meant me harm. The upshot would be that we'd end up really annoyed with each other. I decided to postpone telling him, perhaps forever.

When my phone rang, I thought about not answering it in case it was Tom. But I did, and it wasn't.

"You don't know me," a high-pitched male voice said. "I was a friend of Dilly Friedman. We were in the Six-Pack together."

"Oh, sure," I said. "Which one are you, Brad Kramer or Bob McCauley?"

"I'm Bob McCauley, the Reverend Bob McCauley if you want to use my title."

"Thanks for calling," I said.

There was a pause. Then he said, "I take it I got to you before Brad did. That's unusual. He always used to be at least one step ahead of the rest of us."

He didn't sound happy about having done something faster than Kramer. He didn't sound happy at all. If I had to make a judgment, admittedly based on nothing but the tone of his voice, I'd say he was depressed. "What can I do for you, Reverend McCauley?"

"How about calling me Bob? It's okay. Even my parishioners do."

I turned over and got caught in the top sheet, which had twisted around my legs. As I wrestled it off, I heard McCauley say, "Are you there?"

"I'm here," I said, giving the sheet a final kick. "You still haven't told me why you called."

"I wanted to talk to you about Dilly Friedman. Mrs. Pearl told me that you were interested in learning about her life."

"Yes, that's right, especially the five years after she graduated."

"I don't really know about those years. It was during the ones before, when we were in school, that we were close—very close." I heard him take a deep breath and exhale it. He said, " 'They told me, Heraclitus, they told me you were dead.' "

At first, I was confused. What did somebody named Heraclitus have to do with anything? Then I recognized the quote. It was from a lovely old poem, a lament for a dead friend. I couldn't wait to tell my father that all those English courses I'd taken had turned out to be useful after all. "Right," I said.

"She was a terrific girl." His voice sank. "I can't understand why anyone would have killed her."

"That's too bad, Bob. I was hoping you could."

I heard him gasp over the phone. "What do you mean? Why would you think that?"

I would have sworn he sounded panicked. I wished I could see his face. "Just that you knew her quite well, and I knew her only a little. I had my fingers crossed that you had some information about her that I don't have, something that might explain why she's dead."

"Oh no, I don't. Certainly not. She was a very good person. Nobody could have had a reason to kill her. I mean, there's no reason to kill *anybody*, is there? But especially not Dilly."

I definitely wanted to see this guy. Unless he was a hard-core neurotic, Dilly's death had apparently made a nervous wreck out of him. "Reverend McCauley, are you going to let me meet you? I'd like to talk with you about Dilly."

"We are talking, Ms. Crowne."

"Call me Rachel, and I meant face-to-face."

He sighed. It was the kind of sigh made by someone toting heavy burdens. "Do you really think that's necessary? I have a lot of duties, a lot of responsibilities. You can't imagine what's involved in being the pastor of a church."

"It isn't necessary," I said, "but it would help because I don't have a strong mental picture of you. It makes it hard for me to connect with you."

There was silence on the other end of the line. I waited. "Truthfully, Rachel, I don't understand your involvement in this."

"I was writing about her," I said. "Then she was killed. I'd like to find out why."

His voice got sharper. "You mustn't believe I had anything to do with her murder. I didn't know she was dead until Jim Cohen called and told me and said I should go to the memorial service for her in Fairfield."

"Well, then."

"I just want to talk with you."

There was silence. I waited. He said, "Do you know 'The Ballad of Reading Gaol?' It's by Oscar Wilde."

"I know it."

"Do you remember the refrain?"

"Sure. 'For each man kills the thing he loves, but each man does not die.' Something like that."

"That's it. None of us is without sin, Rachel."

I didn't understand what he was getting at. "Are you saying that you killed Dilly after all."

In went the breath again. "Of course not."

I had a hunch. I said, "Did you love her?"

Again, there was silence. He broke it by saying, "I love all of God's creatures."

"Yeah, sure. Let me ask you again if you loved her."

"Do you mean romantically? Perhaps I did, a little. She was one of the most lovable people I've ever met. Did you say you saw her?"

"Only once."

"She was pretty. Maybe not exactly pretty—I know Brad never thought she was—but attractive. She was full of life. It was a crime to extinguish that life."

I said, "Are you certain you wouldn't like to meet with me? It would be so much easier for us to talk. Where do you live?"

"In Purvis. That's where my church is, Newly Methodist. The people aren't quite what I was used to, but they're nice. Have you ever been to Purvis, Ms. Crowne?"

"Yes, I've been there." That had been awhile ago, and I couldn't remember why I had gone. What I did remember was that it was a mainly working-class area. There was probably some big money there, but most of the people were lower-middle to middle-class economically and lived in little houses with even smaller backyards. They tended to frequent the local bars and restaurants for entertainment rather than go to Fels Point or the Inner Harbor, which were yuppier.

I hadn't spoken to Bob McCauley long enough to form a worthwhile opinion of him, but I had a feeling that he wasn't quite what the locals expected—not if he quoted William Cory and Oscar Wilde with any regularity.

"Would you mind my asking what denomination you are, Ms. Crowne?"

"I'm Jewish."

"Jewish. Really? Crowne doesn't sound Jewish. I . . . I hope you know what I mean."

"I do. My mother said the family name was Cohen, but when my great-grandfather came to this country, the immigration officials changed it. That used to happen a lot."

"That's shocking."

"I agree," I said. "It wouldn't happen now."

"Dilly was Jewish also. The others were, too, except Dicky Miller and me. Do you know Dicky?"

"I met him."

"Yes, he was a bit different from us. I guess that's to be expected, though."

"Why's that?"

"Well, he is a musician."

I thought the whole crew of them, the ones I'd met so far, were "different." Being or not being a musician didn't appear to have anything to do with it. However, I didn't feel I should share this thought with the reverend. "I'd still like to make an appointment to see you," I said.

"Ms. Crowne, do you really believe I killed Dilly?"

"I don't believe anything one way or the other. I just want to talk with you."

He said, "I'm busy the rest of this week. I have to polish my Sunday sermon. I doubt you realize what a chore it is coming up with something new every Sunday, especially if you're trying to reach your people and not succeeding very well. Can this wait until next week?"

"I guess so."

"I don't know," he said. "Maybe I shouldn't wait. I wouldn't want you to speak to Brad first."

Again, I heard the panic. What was this guy afraid of?

"Why not?"

"Why not? I just wouldn't. There are things that need to be said, Rachel, that should have been said five years ago. Maybe it's too late now. With Dilly dead, I guess it is too late. But, still, I want to say them."

I thought about all the murder mysteries I'd read in which someone has something vital to tell. He puts it off, gets killed, and nobody knows what it was. I said, "Say them now."

Silence. Then McCauley said, "No, not now. You were right; we need to see each other face-to-face. Could you meet me next Wednesday for lunch? There's a little restaurant near my church, The Crab. It's nothing fancy, but it has some good food. We can speak privately there."

"I can do that."

He gave me the address of the place, then said, "Ms. Crowne, Rachel, you don't know how happy you've made me."

"Why is that?"

"Let me put it like this. My mother once told me that she thought she had cancer. She knew she needed to find out one way or the other, but she couldn't bring herself to go to the doctor. Finally, she told her best friend, who forced her to go. You could be my best friend, Rachel."

"Could you say that a little plainer?"

"Plainer? Okay. You could force me to face my cancer. I need to do that. Even if the verdict is death, it would be worth it to get what I know off my chest."

He wanted to confess to something. It sounded like I was finally going to get substantial information concerning Dilly's murder. I couldn't wait.

"Anytime, anyplace," I said. "I'm ready to hear what you have to say."

"I'll tell you next Wednesday, as we planned."

"Listen," I said. "You take good care of yourself in the meanwhile."

CHAPTER
16

I exercised hard the next day for about an hour and a half. I needed to work off my accumulated tensions. Still full of energy after that but a lot calmer, I decided to call Murray Rothman, Dilly's former boyfriend. If, as Tom mentioned earlier, the guy had recently had a hernia operation, it was certain he'd be home, barely moving.

I thought this because I remembered my grandfather recuperating from his hernia operation. I think it took him six weeks to get over it.

Rothman's number was in the phone book. I called him. "Hi," I said. "I'm Rachel Crowne. I'm writing an article about Dilly Friedman. I'd like to interview you for it."

"She's dead," he said, his voice strained.

"I know that. This is kind of a commemorative article. I won't take much of your time. Please."

"I don't want to. I hadn't seen her for almost a year before she . . . she . . ." His voice broke. "Oh, hell. Okay, as long as it's pretty quick."

"I promise."

He said, "I'll meet you at the Burger King."

"How can you do that? Didn't you recently have an operation? I remember when my grandfather—"

"It's not like that anymore," he said. "They get you out of the hospital, up and around fast."

"I can be there in twenty minutes," I said.

"Fine."

When I went outside, I saw that it was somewhat over-cast. The sky was that more-gray-than-blue color it usu-ally is around here. I thought wistfully of California and sunshine, then forgot about west of the Rockies. I really enjoyed living in Fairfield, and except for one freaky but harmless little earthquake, which didn't repeat itself, we never had cataclysms of nature here.

The ride to the restaurant was short. I went from Millerville Parkway, to Burden's Parkway, stayed on that for about a mile, then turned into the Burger King lot. It was full. I had to leave my car in back.

I had never been in that restaurant before. Fast-food places aren't my style, mainly because they tend to give me indigestion. The place was crawling with little chil-dren. They took turns crying. A few times, I think, all the kids in there under the age of six or seven cried at once. After consideration, I thought Rothman might have chosen it because it was impossible for anyone else to overhear our conversation.

I spotted him as soon as he came in. He was the only one, besides me, unaccompanied by a kid. He had brown eyes and sparse, dark brown hair. He looked to be about thirty-five. He might have been younger; baldness often makes a guy look older. He was of medium height and thin, with a clear, if sallow, complexion. And nervous. At first, I thought it might be because he didn't want to talk about Dilly. Later, when he didn't get any calmer, I decided he just was that way.

When we got settled, each with a Coke in front of us, I said, "What can you tell me about Dilly?"

He fingered his straw. "What can I tell you? She was a nice girl."

"Yes. That's what everyone says."

"It's true. She was good to everybody and kindhearted."

"So why did you two break up?"

The straw was in his mouth now. He was chewing on it. I wanted to pull it out and stick it back in his cup, but managed to control myself. He chewed a while longer before taking the mangled remains out of his mouth. "Those things happen," he said.

"But for a reason. Tell me why."

He took his tie between two of his fingers and felt it. He was dressed in a brown suit that didn't fit very well and a cream-colored shirt. The tie was brown. I wanted to tell him he was a Winter and should never wear brown. I clamped my lips together.

"It's personal."

"Tell me anyway," I said.

His right eye twitched. "I don't owe you anything. Truthfully, I don't think I like you. You're not my type. You've got a personality like my ex-mother-in-law's bull terrier."

I ignored the compliment. "What is your type?"

He sighed. "Dilly was my type. At least, I thought she was."

I said, "What changed your mind?"

"Don't you ever quit?"

"No," I said, "so let's not waste time. Tell me."

He rubbed his right thumb and first finger together as though trying to knock off a piece of dirt he'd picked up. "She didn't . . . I guess she didn't find me appealing."

I took a sip of soda. "In what way?"

"All ways. She broke up with me."

He sat back and sighed. "She liked my little girl, though. To tell the truth, I think she liked Emily more than me. Maybe that's even why she went with me as long as she did, to be with Emily, I mean."

This reminded me of my initial attraction to Jordan

Goldman. Of course, Jordan was handsome and self-possessed, too, while this guy was neither. I won't deny, though, that his two kids played a strong part in what appealed to me about him. My reason for doting on other people's children was that I couldn't have my own. I wondered what Dilly's reason had been.

Murray gnawed on his lip while I thought about that. Finally, he burst out, "You don't suspect me of murdering her, do you?"

I remembered Tom telling me about the guy's perfect alibi. I said, "No, I don't, but somebody did it. Who do you think it was?"

"Why are you asking me? I don't know. I didn't even know her friends. We went out alone all the time, or with Emily."

"Did Dilly ever talk about any of her friends?"

He started to shake his head, then said, "We did meet one of them at a restaurant we went to here in Fairfield. The guy grabbed her arm as we went by his table. She didn't seem happy to see him. In fact, she looked kind of sick."

"Do you remember his name?"

"No. I just remember he was nice-looking and had a lot of hair."

Rothman's description didn't fit Dicky Miller because he wasn't good-looking. Jim Cohen was. He also had a lot of hair.

"Was this individual blond?"

"Maybe. No, I don't think so. I don't know."

I thought about the third guy at the memorial service, the one who hadn't recited a poem. As I recalled him, he was very good-looking. He had lots of hair, too. It was dark.

I said, "Did he say anything to her?"

"He said something like, 'How you doing, Dilly?

Everything okay?' She acted very cheerful with him and said sure, but I could tell she was upset. She couldn't even eat her dinner. When I asked her about him, she said they used to pal around together in college. I figured, though, he was an old boyfriend, because she seemed so emotional about seeing him." Rothman studied me for a moment or two. "To tell the truth, I didn't see how she could interest a guy like him for long."

"Why is that?" I said.

His face turned red. I didn't know people did that anymore. "He was young," he said. "About Dilly's age. You know how those young guys are."

"Tell me."

"Hot. Hungry. Sex is important to them. Maybe that's all they think about when they're that age."

From my experience, the guys I was acquainted with thought about it at any age. I decided to keep that to myself. "I don't know what you're saying. Why wouldn't Dilly have interested someone like that?"

"Well, because . . ."

I waited.

"Okay," he said. "You want to hear it, I'll tell you. She was frigid. She didn't like sex. I had to practically beg her every time I wanted it. And she never . . . she didn't . . . I don't think she ever got any pleasure out of it. I could tell. I'm not a sexed-up guy particularly, but I got tired of her frigidity after a while. That's why I say I don't think she would have lasted long with a young guy."

"Did you ask her what was wrong?"

I was pushing him. I didn't know how long he was going to put up with it.

He sighed. "Sure I did. After a while. I said I figured it was me, and could she tell me what I was doing wrong."

I leaned forward. "What did she say?"

"Who are you, Dr. Ruth?"

"What did she say?"

"She said it wasn't me. She said she was just that way and couldn't help it. Something had happened to make her that way, and she wasn't able to change, not even after years of therapy. At first, I thought she was just trying to put the blame on herself so as not to hurt my feelings. Dilly would have done that. Then I realized she was really sad about it. I felt sorry for her."

"Is that why you kept seeing her?"

His face reddened again. "I don't think you'd understand, a girl like you."

"What do you mean?"

"You're very attractive—brown curls, blue eyes, a nice figure." He looked at my loose clothes. "I think you have a nice figure."

"So?"

He was rubbing his thumb and first finger together again. "Look at me. Not much, huh. I felt honored that Dilly went out with me. I've been losing my hair since I was twenty-five. She was pretty good-looking. She had a fabulous body. My girlfriends tend not to be so great to be seen with. I guess you could call them dogs. Dilly wasn't. Also, she was lively and fun. I'm not. She was out of my league."

This guy had one of the worst self-images I'd ever come across. I didn't know what to say to him.

I realized he was talking. "I'm sorry. I didn't hear you."

"I said, a girl like you wouldn't go for someone like me. You're out of my league, too. Pretty girls go out with handsome men and vice versa. Unless the guys are rich, like Aristotle Onassis. Being rich makes even ugly guys like him attractive. Do you think Jackie Kennedy would have married him if he hadn't been so rich?"

Although I didn't feel the need to defend Jackie Kennedy, I wanted to explain a theory I had, because this was something I had thought about, too, and been intrigued by. I said, "It's more than that. It's the power, not just the money. Money makes guys feel and act powerful, and power is very, very sexy."

"I don't understand."

"No, most men don't pick up on that, but you can trust me. I'm right." I felt sure I was, since I'd had a few encounters of that kind myself, and I didn't even appreciate arrogance. In fact, I couldn't stand it.

Murray tentatively put out his hand and touched mine. "Would you go out with me?"

I started to say, "What kind of a dog do you think I am?" but it was apparent to me that he didn't have any sense of humor, not about stuff like that anyway. I said, as gently as I could, "I already have a boyfriend. He wouldn't like it."

"Sure," he said, but I could tell he didn't believe me.

CHAPTER
17

I couldn't stop thinking about my conversation with Murray Rothman, specifically his remark that Dilly had been frigid. I had never paid much attention to the subject of frigidity because it wasn't even remotely one of my problems. Now I wondered if there was any truth to some people's belief that it was a result of experience rather than something innate, like not caring for ice cream even when you were a little kid.

If it was environmental, what had caused it in Dilly? The obvious answer was that she'd been raped. If she had been, it seemed to me I had found an important missing piece of the murder puzzle.

I called Tom at his house, told him about my conversation with Rothman, and gave him my conclusion. "It's possible," he said, making me angry because he didn't sound enthusiastic about my idea.

"Ah, come on," I said. "It's more than possible, and you know it."

He sighed into the phone. "You keep forgetting this isn't my case. I don't know anything about it."

"Thanks," I said, "and never mind. I'll find out for myself." I hung up the receiver.

My statement wasn't bravado. I did think I had a chance to get the information. That was because I had a contact at the University of Maryland, where I felt sure that if Dilly had been raped while she was a student, there would be a record of it.

The phone rang. I figured it was Tom again and didn't pick it up. Instead, I went out the door fast. It was Saturday, and I had planned to drive to Baltimore to get Cleome. I didn't see any reason to change my plans. It wouldn't do her any harm to go with me to the university. As I started down the street, I looked over at Tom's house. He had come outside and was waving his arms at me. I didn't stop.

I picked up my young friend, then took her back to my house, where she changed into one of the outfits Nancy had bought her. This was a blue-and-white-checkered top with blue slacks. I thought she looked beautiful. From the way she'd glanced at my polo shirt and old gray slacks, she didn't think I did, but I could live with that.

"How come we're going to the un-i-ver-si-ty?" Cleome said, as though it were impossible to make such a long word intelligible without pausing after each syllable.

I said, "I know somebody there who works in one of the offices. If I can't get anything from the officials, I'm hoping she can give me some information to help me find Miss Friedman's killer."

"That's good," she said, picking up her beloved boom box to take on the trip. "Let's get going."

Cleome and I drove on Route 95, heading to Route 1 and College Park, where the university's main campus was. It was a nice day, or would have been if the road hadn't had so many trucks on it, like the one behind me hauling cement and threatening to overrun me. Also, I had to keep the windows closed and turn on the air conditioning because the exhaust fumes were so bad.

Cleome said, "What's a university anyway?"

"It's a school, a big school, with lots of other schools in it, like a school of education and an agricultural school. It's where Miss Friedman and her five best friends went."

"That's why we want to go there?"

"That's why," I said.

"Did you go to it, too?"

"No, not that one, but I went. I liked it."

"It was a school and you liked it?"

"You bet. That's because it teaches people lots of stuff, and I like learning things. Also, it's pretty much a place where you're your own boss. I like that, too."

"Could it teach me things?"

"Yes, of course. You have to wait till you're older, though, and graduate from high school, so just make sure you do."

"Okay, I'll do that. Let me ask you something else. If you got taught so much, and you're a smart lady, where's your boyfriend?"

That was quite a jump. I wasn't expecting it. Maybe that's why her question rattled me—or maybe it was because I'd been wondering the same thing. "What brought that on?" I said, aware I sounded a little cranky.

Cleome patted my arm. "I've been thinking about that. I know women got four or five men at the same time. Don't seem natural you ain't got one. I guess I worry about you."

I was astonished, and kind of indignant, too. "You worry about me?"

"Yes, ma'am."

"Well," I said, "I do have a boyfriend—sort of—so you can stop worrying."

"Where is he?"

I didn't know where he was, but I didn't want to admit it. Though I'd talked to Jordan on the phone a few times since we'd gotten together that afternoon with Tom, he'd sounded distant. "He's busy," I said.

"Maybe you need someone who ain't so busy."

Maybe I did, but I didn't want to hear it just then. "Thank you for the advice."

"You're welcome."

That was Cleome, always polite. It was nice, except I wished she were not so forthcoming with her opinions sometimes.

She gave me a look. I recognized it. It was the same kind I gave her when I thought I was improving her life. I might entertain the idea that I was Cleome's surrogate mama, but I had a strong suspicion she thought she was mine. The thought was humbling.

I said, "Do you have a boyfriend?"

She shrugged. "No. I've been thinking about it, but I decided I ain't ready. Let you know when I am."

If acquiring a boyfriend meant sex and having a baby, a real possibility in her world, I hoped she would tell me before she did anything irrevocable. I'd do everything in my power to talk her out of it.

I wished she had a more responsible mother. On the other hand, the "bad" me whispered in my head, maybe if her mother were wonderful, Cleome wouldn't need me. A bit ashamed of myself, I was glad Jews believed only bad acts, not thoughts, counted against them.

It was too nice a day to bother about problems. I decided to change the subject. "Notice how the landscape is different?" I asked. "That's because we're on Route One now."

"What's a landscape?"

When I explained, she said, "Yeah. They got a bunch of little stores here, like where I live."

It was true, though I might not have made the connection. That's because Route 1 near College Park wasn't as run-down as the streets leading to Cleome's place. Here the doughnut shops, palm reader joints, and taco carry-outs were only semiderelict.

We swung into the campus, and the scene changed again. Now there was one redbrick building after another, all, even the nuclear engineering one, trying to pretend they were there from colonial days. A lot of students were milling about. Every one of the kids I saw looked like hell, long hair on both sexes, sweats, ill-fitting jeans, and huge tops that would have fit Shaquille O'Neal, except for the kids who were wearing shorts and barely any tops at all. Cleome pointed to a group who were wearing the sloppy outfits. "They've got clothes like you," she said.

By God, she was right. I wondered if I was a case of arrested development. "Thanks," I said.

"You're welcome."

I kept driving, looking for a place to park. There were maybe a million parking lots, but they were all restricted to students or faculty. Finally, at the opposite end of the campus from where I'd pulled in, I spotted a public lot. Serendipitously, it was next to the Verifications Office, where the registrar plied his trade.

I wasn't sure he'd want to see us, but there was no trouble. A secretary ushered us in, and a genial-looking man rose from behind his desk and shook our hands. His nameplate said he was Mr. Guzmán.

"I'm investigating the murder of a former U. of Maryland student," I said. "I was wondering if you could give me any information on her while she was here. In fact, I need information on the five guys she hung out with at the university, too."

He cleared his throat. "Is this an official request?"

I was afraid he'd ask that. "Not really," I said. "I'm a

writer investigating her murder." I showed him my business card.

Guzmán looked toward Cleome and smiled. She was wearing her solemn face and didn't smile back. You would never have known she had dimples. He said, "Is she a fellow writer?"

I laughed. "No, she was a student of the woman I'm interested in. Cleome wants to know who murdered her, too."

Mr. Guzmán shook his head regretfully. "I'm afraid I can't tell either of you anything. Since 1974, there's been a law on the books that restricts information we can give out. I could give you her dates of attendance and whether or not she graduated from here, but I'm afraid that's all without her written permission."

"You ain't going to get that," Cleome said, giving him a look that clearly said he was somebody's fool. "Didn't you hear Miss Rachel say she's dead?"

"Yes. I'm sorry."

I said, "Just for the sake of discussion, if I had her consent, what could you tell me from her records?"

"What I have here. I could tell you individual grades she got. Some companies, for example, don't care if a student got an A in music appreciation and swimming. They want to know how he did in his computer courses."

"Okay," I said. "Let me ask you another thing. Suppose something happened on this campus, a crime, that the person I'm interested in saw. Her name was Delilah Friedman, by the way." Mr. Guzmán wrote this down. Then he asked me for her major and the date she graduated. I don't know why he bothered since, as Cleome pointed out, we weren't going to get Dilly's permission to examine her records. I wondered if it would count if her brother approved our request. Then I decided not to concern myself about that. The police must have had all this stuff already. If I couldn't do this myself, I'd take another shot at Tom.

I said, "Getting back to what I was asking you, suppose she'd seen a crime committed while she was still a student, or been the victim of one. Would there be a record of that?"

Mr. Guzmán leaned back in his chair. I was far enough away from him to see that he was jiggling his right leg. I wondered why so many men do that. It seems that they can't keep still; they always have to be moving something. I'd ask Tom; he did it, too.

The registrar must have seen me staring at his leg, because he stopped shaking it. "There would be a record," he said, "but it wouldn't be here. It would be kept in a section called Security Records. That's in the Security Office."

Bingo. That was where my friend worked.

I must have looked enthusiastic because Mr. Guzmán shook his head. "You'd never get access to anything there."

"How are the records kept?" I asked.

"They're in an electronic database. But an unauthorized person wouldn't be able to get into it."

She would if her friend ran off a copy for her. I tried not to look smug.

Mr. Guzmán started to rise but sat down again when I said I had just a few more questions. He said okay and didn't even glance at his watch. Nice guy.

"Suppose she had witnessed something bad here and reported it. Would the police have been called?"

The leg started jiggling again. "We don't really have a police force. We depend on the College Park police for anything serious, and, yes, they would have been called."

"Thank you very much," I said. This time I extended my hand first. I heard Cleome repeat my words, but she didn't put her hand out. I had a feeling she wasn't too crazy about pressing the flesh with white guys. In her world, a girl never knew when one of them might turn on somebody black. In fact, it was amazing that she'd trusted Dilly and me. She must have had an instinct for who was practically guaranteed to be okay.

I pulled back my wandering thoughts and, after getting directions from a guy at the information desk, steered us over to the Security Office. We were lucky. My friend was at the front desk.

Actually, she wasn't my friend. She had a longtime crush on my brother David, who was still in Israel, and I was betting she'd cooperate in the hope that he'd like her better if she did.

Her name was Sally Steinmetz, age about twenty-four. She had dark hair and a pleasant rather than pretty face. Sally was a big-boned girl, which in David's eyes was already one strike against her. He liked them little and cuddly, whereas she could have engulfed him in her paws. Also, she wasn't very smart. To David, that was a big problem also. In fact, it was the biggest.

I decided it was only right to tell her that what I was going to ask wasn't my brother's idea and, in fact, he probably wouldn't approve. "Ask anyway," she said, her eyes sparkling with excitement. I think it was brought on by the mention of David's name. She added, "I can always say no."

"I'd like to see the security file on Delilah Friedman." I said she'd been an education major and gave the date she'd graduated.

Sally said no.

So take that, David, I thought. You're not such a lady-killer after all.

"I want to help," she rushed on. "Really, I do, but it

would mean my job to give you private information. Can't you get—what's her name—Friedman to give you written approval? That would make it all right."

I explained why that wouldn't happen.

Sally looked as though she were about to cry. "That's so sad," she said. "I'd like to help you. I really would. But I can't." Her expression became pensive. Cleome and I stood there. Then her face brightened. "Listen," she said, "I know I shouldn't say this, but you could always get someone to break into the files. A good hacker could do it."

"A hacker," I said. "Do you know one?"

She shook her head.

Where was I going to find a hacker?

Cleome said, "Does he hack people? I might be able to find someone around where I live. Of course, it could take awhile."

Sally looked confused. I tried not to laugh and managed a fairly well-controlled grin. Still, I'd have to talk to Cleome about her late-night movie viewing. For the present, I said, "Thank you, hon, but not just yet."

Again, I asked myself where I was going to find a hacker. I stared to walk out of the office, Cleome trailing behind me. I didn't say good-bye to Sally because I had forgotten about her. I didn't remember until she called out, "Give my love to David."

"David," I said. "Yes, sure."

When we got back to the house, I called Nancy Martin. I said, "I need a hacker to break into a secret file at the University of Maryland. Can you get me somebody?"

"Why do you want to do that? Does it have to do with the death of that Friedman woman?"

"Sure does."

"All right, I'll get you someone. It might take a few days, though. I'm a bit busy."

"You know I'm asking you to help me in something illegal."

"Of course I know."

"Just out of curiosity, does that bother you any?"

She laughed. "Why would it?"

"I was just wondering."

"Don't be absurd. If I'm involved, it can't be wrong."

"Stupid me," I said, "not to have thought of that."

CHAPTER
18

Another Monday. Somebody was leaning on my bell. That irritated me; I don't like noise. I ran to the door and said in an angry voice, "Who is it?" I didn't get a response, but at least the ringing stopped.

Peering through the peephole, I saw a very good-looking guy, probably in his late twenties. He had brown hair, which had obviously been styled by an expert, and brown eyes, with lashes most of the women I knew would have killed for. I asked him again to identify himself; after all that had been happening, there was no way I was going to open the door without finding out who he was and what he wanted.

"It's Brad Kramer," he said, "Dilly's old college friend. I heard you want to talk to me." Still at the peephole, I caught the edge of an ingratiating smile. After I let him in, I thought about asking him why he hadn't called to tell me he was coming. Then I decided not to bother. He was here, and I did want to talk to him.

I studied him more thoroughly. The overall impression he made was of someone with excellent taste and the money to express it. His blue suit was cut narrow both in the jacket and the pants, the way continental clothes are, and he was lean enough to look good in it. His shirt was a blue-and-white-striped cotton with a white collar. His tie was a power yellow. His watch, I noticed, was a Rolex.

I observed, too, that his nails were manicured. Believe it or not, I'd never been married to or even gone out with a guy who had his nails done. Brad Kramer was a new experience.

While I was giving him the once-over, he was doing the same to me. Dressed, as usual, to go running, biking, clean a cesspool, or otherwise engage in sweaty activity, I wasn't exactly an example of haute couture. It didn't take him long to dismiss me as an acceptable member of the human race, though I could tell he tried to be circumspect about it.

Then he looked around my family room. Apparently, he found that inadequate as well.

I told myself not to be defensive. Why should I care what he thought of me and my house? I said as pleasantly as I could manage, "Thanks for coming."

He grinned, revealing terrific teeth. I'd have bet anything they were capped. Nature didn't do it that well. He said, "Since you want to talk to me, maybe I can do something for you—clear up questions, that kind of thing. I'd be happy to."

He had a nice speaking voice, low-pitched and sincere. I said, "Fine. Who told you I wanted to talk to you?"

One shoulder went up. "I can't remember. It could have been several people. Mind if I sit?" He didn't wait for an answer. Instead, he scanned the chair he'd chosen.

I said, "What are you looking for? I'm all out of cockroaches and rodents, also crickets, though I could probably scare up some dust mites."

His smile was engaging. He said, "I'm sorry. I didn't mean to be insulting. Scrutinizing things must be a habit of mine. I'd make a good detective, I guess." He sat, then adjusted the knees of his suit with his pretty fingernails. "Here I am, so what do you want to ask me?"

"I'm interested in your relationship with Dilly Friedman."

He shook his head. "I don't have one."

"But you did."

He looked around the room, then back at me. "That was five years ago. My dealings with her ended when we graduated from the University of Maryland."

"Dealings." That was an interesting word. It made their friendship sound like a business. I took the seat across from him. "Why was that?"

He gave me a surprised look. "We didn't have anything in common anymore. She was going to be a teacher. I was on my way up."

"Up? Where's up?" I asked.

"You know, entering the corporate world, advancing. She wasn't interested in that, but I was. I guess I've always been."

"So, did you?"

"Did I what?"

"Advance?"

He smiled. "You could say that. I work for the Major Food Company. You've heard of it, right?"

Of course I had. It was the biggest supermarket chain in the East. I nodded.

"Right now I'm in the advertising department, midlevel, but that won't last much longer."

"Oh? Why not?"

This time the grin burst forth like the finale to a fireworks display on the Fourth of July. "Because I'm engaged to Mr. Hunt's daughter. In case you don't know, he's the president of Major."

"Being engaged to his daughter is good for your career, huh?"

"Is being the Queen of England good?"

"Not at present," I said. "She's got a lot of problems."

"Yeah. Well, I don't." He put up his right hand. "I don't want you to get me wrong, though. The way I put it, you might be wondering if I love her—Mr. Hunt's daughter, that is."

"I was, kind of."

"Well, of course I do. She's very sweet. But even if I didn't, it would be okay. I plan to treat her well."

"That's nice of you."

"It's also smart." His voice had become self-appreciative. "See, Mr. Hunt cares too much about Irene and her comfort to have her be married to a midlevel guy. She's his only child. I figure I could be a vice president in five years, maybe less. That's not bad, is it?"

"Depends on what you want," I said. "It wouldn't interest me."

Once again, his glance slid over the contents of my room. "I guess not. I'm different, though. I've always meant to be rich, and I'm going to be, even earlier than I'd planned. There's nothing wrong with that, is there?"

I shrugged, then got back to the business at hand. "Did Dilly think there was anything wrong with it?"

"Oh, Dilly. She was like you, not materialistic. I never understood that. What else is there?"

"I can think of lots of things."

He tilted his head. "I've disappointed you, haven't I?"

"Me? I never had any expectations for you, so I could hardly be disappointed. Did you disappoint Dilly?"

The good nature, the air of wanting to please, was evaporating like fog in strong sunlight. "Why would you think that? Has anybody been talking to you? I'll bet it was that dumb Bob McCauley."

I said, "I did speak to him. He seems to be upset about

something. Was there anything that happened between you and Dilly that would do that to him?"

"Me and Dilly? Why are you singling me out? How about all of us and Dilly?"

Oh boy, I was definitely onto something. "Okay," I said, trying not to sound excited. "How about all of you and her?"

He gave me a sullen look. "I don't know what you mean. And if I were you, I wouldn't listen to Bob. He's neurotic as hell, not to mention being overwrought most of the time."

"Is that so? What made him get like that?"

He shifted his long legs, this time not bothering to smooth the fabric of his pants. "How should I know?"

"Why don't you take a guess?"

He hesitated. "All right. What I think is that he's dissatisfied being a minister. I think he thought he would love it—you know, taking care of the seekers after spirituality and that kind of stuff—but I don't believe he does. He's always complaining about being worked to death. Plus he says his parishioners, or whatever they're called, don't seem to like him much."

Brad's laugh was condescending. "Of course they don't. He's too highbrow for them. He recites poetry. He's done it as long as I've known him. How many people, especially in a place like Purvis, are going to go for that?"

"Maybe he'll move up, too," I said, "find a congregation that's more highbrow."

"Not if he doesn't keep his mouth shut."

I was on him like a tiger on a staked goat, speaking figuratively, of course. "About what? Tell me what you mean."

He stood. Was he going to leave? I said, "Sit down, please. We're not finished."

He glared at me. Mr. Going-to-Marry-the-Boss's-Daughter didn't expect to be talked to that way. He sat, though.

"Look." His expression grew mild, his voice placating. This guy was a chameleon. "You seem to think I'm a bad person. I'm not. I like Bob, and I love Irene. I'll make her a good husband. Mr. Hunt won't have anything to complain about."

We were back to Mr. Hunt. I said, "I'm relieved about that. I'm sure his daughter will be, too."

His face wrinkled in distaste. I had a feeling Brad Kramer didn't like me much. "You know what I mean," he said.

There was silence while we both stared at each other. Then he said, "I'm an ambitious guy, Rachel. I don't make any bones about it; I'm not a hypocrite. Mr. Hunt knows it, and he likes that about me; he said so. That's because he's the same way. See, I've always meant to get to the top, and now I'm guaranteed to. Naturally, I'm concerned about Mr. Hunt. He's the key to my future."

"I hope you and he will be very happy."

"You don't approve of me, do you?"

"Does it matter?"

He shifted in his chair. "Certainly, it does. I'm not in the business of making enemies."

He started to say something else, but I held up my hand. "I really want to talk about you and Dilly," I said, "not you and your devotion to the daughter of Mr. Moneybags."

I could see the struggle in his face. Part of him wanted to act offended, although I'd begun to doubt that anything could truly get through to him. The other part wanted to hear what I had to say about Dilly. The other part won. He said, "Okay, let's start over. What do you want to know?"

"I want to know what happened around graduation time that affected Dilly adversely."

"Adversely?"

"Yes. Something happened that turned her into a kind of recluse. It must have been a terrible thing to have changed her so much. I think it might have affected Everett Pearl, too."

He sighed. "Yeah, Everett. He committed suicide. I consider that a mark of weakness. Don't you?"

"I thought he died from an accidental overdose of pain medication."

"Did his mother tell you that? That's what she tells everybody. That's not what I heard, though. I think he killed himself because he couldn't face starting a new life. That makes him a weakling, doesn't it?"

I tried not to sound as indignant as I felt. "I don't consider suicide like that. I generally consider it a response to depression."

"That's weakness, isn't it?"

I definitely did not like this man. "It's sad," I said.

He laughed. "Spoken like a woman."

"I'd say it was spoken like a feeling person. You ought to try being one someday."

His face turned red. I'd drawn blood. I was delighted.

Not waiting for him to recoup, I said, "Now tell me why Bob needs to keep his mouth shut."

He seemed to struggle with himself. Then he said, "Okay. I'll be straight with you. Anything to get you off my back. Something happened graduation night that shouldn't have. We were all drinking. That included Dilly. Everett kept telling her to stop. We all knew she couldn't hold her liquor. She didn't listen, though. Even you would have to agree that it was just as much her fault as it was any of the rest of us."

"What was her fault?"

"What happened. In fact, to tell you the truth, I don't think it was our fault, the guys' fault, I mean. It's a woman's responsibility to stay in control. Don't you agree?"

Before I could answer, undoubtedly with words that wouldn't have made him happy, he said, "Irene would never do anything like that. If she did, I'd stop her."

"But you didn't stop Dilly."

Again I got the surly look. "Why was it my job to do that? Besides, Everett kept telling her and it didn't do any good. She'd listen to him before she'd listen to me."

"She let you make love to her," I said. "Maybe she let all of you make love to her."

He started to laugh. "Boy, are you on the wrong track."

"Okay," I said. "How about this scenario? One of the Six-Pack was driving the car you were all in. Maybe it was Dilly. The person clipped somebody, ran over somebody, maybe even killed somebody, and you've all been covering up ever since—and maybe worrying she'd spill the beans and ruin all your chances for success. Finally, one of you worried so much, you killed her."

He leaned toward me, renewed confidence all over his face. "You're a writer, huh? You must write fantasy. Nobody ran over anyone, not even a squirrel."

"Then tell me," I said.

He leaned back again, obviously at ease. "I don't think so. I want you to figure it out. Why should I make it easy for you?"

I tried to keep the temper out of my voice. "If I do, will you let me know when I'm right?"

The tension was back. "Are you crazy?"

I stood up and got close to him. I wished I were physically intimidating like Tom, but that wasn't going to happen. "You'd better tell me," I said. "Otherwise the police might be asking you these questions. I bet you wouldn't play games with them."

He gave me a contemptuous look. Interesting how he'd changed from the guy who at first only wanted to be agreeable. "I've already talked to the police. They don't have anything on me."

I walked toward the door, then wheeled around and fixed him with an unfriendly stare. "I've got another idea," I said. "How about if I tell Mr. Hunt that you're under suspicion of murder because of something that happened—something you did—five years ago? Do you think the president of Major Food and the father of little Irene is going to like that?"

He stood, too. His face contorted. "I'll sue your ass off."

"Not without revealing what you're implicated in, you won't. I wouldn't think Mr. Hunt would like that, either. From what I've heard about him, even the faintest hint of scandal would turn him against you."

Naturally, I was making this up, since I hadn't even known of Mr. Hunt's existence before Brad came to my house. It appeared to affect Kramer, however, if his shaking hands meant anything.

"Would you really do that?"

"If necessary."

"Will you leave me alone if I tell you?"

I said, "It depends on what you tell me."

"Okay," he said. "Graduation night we had sex with her—we didn't make love to her; that's a joke. She was practically unconscious from the alcohol when it happened. She didn't care. She didn't even protest, before or after, so it wasn't rape. Let me repeat that—we didn't rape her. Then we left her."

"You left a drunk, helpless woman? Where? At the university?"

He nodded.

"Why?"

He gave me a quick glance, then turned his face so that he wasn't looking directly at me anymore. "It was like this. Jim Cohen had a new car, a graduation gift. He was afraid if he took her home she'd get sick in it, or on us. She'd already thrown up once. So we left her."

"Everett, too?"

"No, he left earlier in his own car. He didn't like what was going on."

I believed him. Yet something felt wrong, and not just that Everett hadn't turned out to be such a *tsotskala*, after all. Abandoning a semiconscious woman is despicable, not to mention having sex with her, but I wouldn't think it would be a reason to murder her. It was all I had to work with, though. I said, "Did you kill her so she couldn't tell her story and mess up your chance for advancement?"

For a moment, I saw a glimpse of something ugly in his expression. Then it was gone. "Me, kill someone?" he said with a jaunty smile. "Rachel, Rachel, I'm surprised at you. You ought to know that I don't need to resort to murder to keep a woman in line. I have other ways." He moved close to me. I felt his warm, minty breath on my cheek. I would have backed off, but the wall was behind me. "Would you like to see a few?"

"I don't think so," I said. "I find you really boring."

He didn't like that. I'd dented his ego. "I was kidding about putting the move on you," he said. "You're not the least bit desirable. You should look at yourself in the mirror. Your clothes are terrible and your hair is out of control. I'd be ashamed to be seen with you."

I said, "To paraphrase Judy Garland, I can do something about my appearance anytime I want to, but no matter how you try, you'll still be boring."

I could see him attempting to recover his equilibrium. He wasn't doing a good job. Before our verbal duel escalated, I needed to get him out of my house. "It's been fun," I said, "but you have to go home now. And don't come back."

He didn't say anything for a moment or two. Then he walked to the door, stopped, and turned. "Maybe I won't, but maybe I will. Think about that, Rachel."

I hated his getting in the last word.

CHAPTER
19

I had a headache when I got up the next morning. The headache was from not getting enough sleep; instead of relaxing, I'd been thinking of ways, none of them doable, to put Brad Kramer in his place.

When the phone rang, I jerked it off its cradle and said in an irritated voice, "Yes? Who is it?"

The person on the other end was Nancy. She said, "My, you're in a good mood."

"Is there some reason I should be?"

"Actually, there is. I found a hacker for you, and he'll do the job for nothing."

I've always believed that you get what you pay for, so I could not be as excited about this as she probably expected. I said, "I don't understand. Why would he do it for nothing?"

"He explained it to me. He said he likes to do illegal stuff. It's fun and a challenge."

"Where'd you find this guy, in the local institution for sociopaths? It's probably a good thing I don't need him."

"What do you mean you don't need him?"

"I think I found out yesterday what happened to Dilly five years ago."

"Tell me." Nancy sounded as eager as she ever gets.

"Nonconsensual sex!" I said. My voice rose dramatically. "Dilly may have been involved in nonconsensual sex graduation night."

I wasn't dramatizing the awful event because I didn't care; I cared a lot. It was that being a writer, I never could seem to stop myself from doing that sort of thing. Everything was a story to me, even if it was a horror story.

"Why do you call it that?" Nancy asked. She sounded annoyed. "Are you saying she was raped, or are you saying something else that I don't understand?"

I said, "To call it rape wouldn't be accurate. According to the person who told me what happened, she was too drunk to agree to it or decline."

Nancy said, "Who was she nonconsensual with?"

"I'm not sure if my source is telling the whole truth. It could be some or all of the male members of the Six-Pack."

"That's disgusting. They were supposed to be her friends."

"Right," I said.

I also wondered if Everett Pearl had committed suicide, as Brad had insisted, instead of dying accidentally, as his mother said. He sounded like a sensitive guy, if a possible rapist could ever be considered sensitive. Shame at taking advantage of a drunken girl might have made him do it. Even if he hadn't raped her, shame at abandoning her might have seemed enough of a cause.

I thought about Bob McCauley, the poetry-spouting minister. He was sensitive, too. If he'd been one of the ones who violated Dilly, no wonder he was upset.

More important, who'd killed Dilly? Everett was out, of course; he was already dead when the murder took place. That left four guys. They'd all had something to lose if she talked, even Dicky Miller. I wouldn't think the bus company would want to keep a driver on the payroll who'd been accused of rape. Fairfield was liberal, but not that liberal.

Had one of the four killed her? Maybe all of them had done it together, so that nobody could blackmail them individually.

I said, "When can this hacker break into the system?"

"I thought you said you might not need him."

"I changed my mind. Even if I think I know what happened to Dilly, it would be good to find out what the records say."

"I agree."

"Then that clinches it."

"You really want to tie up this case, don't you?"

"Sure, I do. Besides, I have a feeling about it. I think something is going to happen pretty soon, that we're at a turning point. I'm finally finding out stuff. Maybe what I learn from Dilly's file will give me the information to crack this case."

"Or get you killed."

"Not a chance," I said, willing myself to forget that a person or persons unknown had left a rat and two gruesome dolls outside my door.

There was silence on the other end of the line, until Nancy said, "There *is* a chance, and I think you ought to consider it."

"I can't. You know me. Just tell this hacker to get to work, okay?"

"If that's what you want. I'll call you as soon as I hear anything."

Nancy didn't get back to me until the next day, shortly before I was to meet the Reverend Bob McCauley at the restaurant in Purvis. "Is everything okay?" I said when she called.

"Are you asking if the hacker broke into the system? Yes, he did. He said it was easy. Did he get caught? No, he didn't. We're all safe from jail, at least in the short run. Whether or not they can track him down is something else. I don't know much about these things."

"Encouraging," I said.

Nancy's sigh was surprisingly gloomy. "Nothing else is."

"Don't tell me there wasn't any record."

"There was, but not what you were hoping for. He said the record shows she was discovered outside the building where the dean of students' office is. Her clothes were in disarray and she didn't have on any panties. She said she'd been attacked during an attempted robbery."

"You're kidding."

"No, I'm not. Let me finish. She said she was jumped by two guys she'd never seen before, and they shoved her around. Then they heard someone coming and ran away. When the campus police wanted to take her to the infirmary, she refused. End of story."

So sweet, loving Dilly had protected her friends, even though they didn't deserve it. She was that kind of person.

But, then, why had she been killed five years later, and by whom? It didn't make sense to me that after all that time, someone would start fearing that she'd suddenly begin talking.

So, I still wasn't closer to having an answer to my questions. There were a lot of answers I didn't have. I hoped Bob McCauley would give them to me.

CHAPTER
20

It was raining hard when I went out to my car the next morning. I turned on my windshield wipers, but they didn't do a lot of good. I was going to have to take my time driving to Purvis.

It should have been no more than twenty-five minutes from Fairfield to the other town. Instead, because of the bad weather, it took about forty. A couple of times I thought the car was going to drown. Once, the vehicle next to me skidded and just missed hitting me. Bob McCauley had better make this trip worthwhile for me, I thought.

Purvis was about five miles beyond the Harbor Tunnel. My initial impression was that it was the kind of place most people would rather move from than to. It wasn't so much that it was obviously not well off as that it was dreary in appearance and seemed to have little to offer in the way of amenities.

I drove past row after row of attached small brick houses, most of them with windows capped with aluminum awnings and tiny yards set off from the neighbors' lots by chain-link fences. I saw quite a few churches, too, the majority of them Evangelical Lutheran or Baptist. None of them was Methodist, though I thought I remembered McCauley saying his church was.

The Crab was on the corner of a commercial stretch

made up of maybe six small stores. It looked like a shack, but not a picturesque one. It was painted brown and had a brown roof. I noticed that a number of shingles were missing and wondered if the rain had leaked through to the inside. Also, in spite of the rain, the air around the place smelled greasy. I almost didn't go in. But Bob McCauley was waiting.

The inside of the restaurant didn't look any nicer than the outside, maybe worse. The walls were painted operating-room green, and the floor was green linoleum. There were plenty of cracks in the linoleum as well as some missing sections. I also spotted several puddles on the floor, no doubt from where the roof shingles were missing. A person not paying attention to where she was going could break a leg.

There was a row of wooden booths on one side of the room next to the long windows, tables in the center, and a bar on the far side. There were no more than six or seven people in the place. Bob McCauley was one of them. He was sitting in the last booth with a book propped in front of him. He didn't appear to be reading it. I picked my way carefully around the minefield of a floor, shed my wet raincoat, shook the wet from my hair, and sat down across from him. He seemed startled to see me, as though he hadn't really expected me to show up.

After greeting me in a subdued voice, he said, "I was beginning to worry. The weather is so bad, and you were late, and I was afraid—oh, never mind. I'm happy you're here."

He could have fooled me. I would have said that he looked as though the hounds of Hell were at his heels. I felt sorry for him.

Not sorry enough, though, to refrain from trying to wear him down. He seemed vulnerable, more so than when I'd talked to him on the phone. I needed to work on that vulnerability. I had to, for Dilly's sake—and mine. I intended to finish what I'd started.

"Why don't we decide what we want to eat before we talk," he said, handing me a food-and-coffee-stained menu. I opened it, expecting to find at least four or five crab dishes. Otherwise, why would the place be called The Crab, right? There was one crab dish: a sandwich with lettuce, tomato, and tartar sauce.

"Is this any good?" I asked McCauley, pointing my finger at the entree.

His smile was melancholy. "Not really. It's always full of shells and cartilage and things."

It was the "things" that decided me. I ordered a tuna sandwich and coffee. As though too upset to make an independent decision, McCauley got the same.

He was wearing a wilted white shirt, an unfashionably narrow blue tie, and a brown suit. There was a spot of ketchup on the shirt, and his light-colored hair was mussed. He looked like someone who needed to be taken care of.

I said, "I saw Brad Kramer two days ago. He came to my house."

"Is that so? Uh, what did you two talk about?"

"About Dilly Friedman, of course."

"Oh yes, of course. Did he have much to say? Anything you hadn't heard before?"

"Several things," I said.

"Oh yes? He's quite a guy, isn't he?"

I shrugged.

"Weren't you impressed with him? People usually are. He's a real go-getter, and smart."

"Is that what he is? I'd say he was a user."

As soon as I'd uttered the words, I knew I shouldn't have. From his pained expression, it was apparent that McCauley was loyal to the bone; he couldn't bear to hear anything bad about a friend, especially if it was true. "Of course, I could be wrong," I said.

He looked relieved. "Oh, you are. He's a really nice person once you get to know him. The thing is, he's ambitious. Getting ahead means everything to him. He can't help it."

I said, "You're not like that."

I didn't think his unhappy expression could deepen, but it did. "You're wrong," he said. "I'm ambitious, too. I don't want to stay in Purvis the rest of my life."

Who could blame him? But instead of agreeing with him, I pointed out that he wasn't eating his sandwich. I guess to satisfy me, he picked it up and took a bite. I doubt that he tasted it, though. He seemed too full of despair to have room for anything else.

I said, "What would you have to do to get out of here?"

His laugh lacked humor. "Write articles. Shake a lot of hands and be charming and helpful. Raise money. Volunteer to serve on some of the bishop's committees. And one more thing. I'd need to appear blameless. I mean, truly good. I can't let it seem that I'm a sinner, not in any big way. That would be the end of me."

I put down my tuna fish. "That should be easy. You are good, aren't you?"

He shifted his feet restlessly. "Can we get out of here?" he said. "It's not raining any more. Unless, of course, you'd like some dessert first."

I assured him I didn't, gave in when he insisted with a firmness that surprised me that he pay the whole bill, and walked out with him.

It had stopped raining, but the outside of The Crab hadn't profited from the free wash. It looked as grubby and grimy as it had when I'd gone in. The neighborhood we walked through didn't seem much better. There were more brown brick houses, an American Legion post advertising bingo, two funeral homes converted from residences, and a big food store I'd never heard of. In spite of his rumpled look, Bob McCauley appeared out of place.

I said, "Don't you want to know what Brad Kramer told me, besides the fact that he's marrying the boss's daughter so that he can get a leg up in the corporate world?"

McCauley looked shocked. "Did he actually say that?"

"He didn't have to. He made it clear in a million ways."

"I'm sure he'll treat her well," McCauley said with a sigh.

"That's what he said."

The reverend seemed a little happier.

"Anyway, he told me that you all had sex with Dilly graduation night."

I think if I had taken out a gun and pointed it at McCauley, he couldn't have looked any more shocked. He stopped moving. Staring straight ahead, he said, "He told you that? Are you sure?"

"Of course I'm sure. Was he lying?"

He hesitated. I could almost see him wrestling with himself. Then he turned to face me. "No, he wasn't lying. Well, not exactly. It was . . . it was a mistake. I mean, no one planned it; it wasn't a scheme. It was because of the circumstances. Do you want to hear about it?"

Did I want to be a famous writer and have editors beg me for articles? I said yes.

"We were all drinking, including Dilly. We were doing it for most of the day, I guess, beginning right after the graduation ceremony. Dilly never did have any capacity for alcohol. After a while, she kind of passed out. Maybe she didn't lose consciousness completely—I guess she didn't—but she might as well have. I know she couldn't stand up by herself."

I said, "How convenient for you guys."

His face reddened. "I don't think we hurt her. We didn't even force her much."

I stood up straighter. "What do you mean 'much'?"

"I . . . I guess she didn't really want us to do it, especially the last two of us. She cried."

So Brad had lied to me. "That's rape," I said.

"Yes, it is." His voice was so low I could barely hear him.

Poor Dilly. I wanted to hit him. "Whose idea was it?" I said insistently. "Somebody must have started it."

Bob McCauley seemed reluctant to answer. I persisted. His mouth hardly opening, he said, "It was Jim Cohen. He said it would be a great way to celebrate. It seemed like a wonderful idea at the time. So, everybody did it but Everett."

"Why didn't he?"

I noticed he wasn't looking at me again. "He just didn't."

"Did he try to stop you?"

"I don't remember. All I remember is that I did it. Oh, God, I had sex with a defenseless girl, a friend. Would anyone forgive me? Could you?"

"Me? Why does it matter what I think?"

"It matters, Rachel. Tell me."

I thought about Dilly, about how sweet and caring she'd been. I thought about her vulnerability and how she'd been taken advantage of. I thought about how her personality had changed for the worse after the rape. I said, "Do you want the truth?"

"Yes."

"The answer is no. I wish I could forgive you, but I can't."

"Oh, God. I don't blame you. I don't think I'll ever get over it. I hate myself, Rachel. I'm one of the 'inconsolable self-accused.'"

Distracted, as always, by a telling phrase, I said, "Who wrote that?"

"I don't know, but I can tell you, it describes me."

Despite what I'd said about not forgiving him, I felt genuinely sorry for him. Dilly was beyond help. I wished I could do something for him. "Do you at least feel better for having told me?" I asked.

He shook his head. "How can I? You can't give me absolution even if you would."

"Is that what you want? Why don't you go to your bishop? He can do it, can't he? Or am I thinking of Catholics?"

"No. Methodists believe in the value of confession."

"Well, then, maybe you should talk to him. Or would that end your career?"

"It would end it all right, not that the bishop would say that to me. He'd listen, and he'd tell me I did the right thing in coming to him. Then he'd make sure I'd never get out of Purvis, unless it was to go somewhere worse. The Church may forgive, but it doesn't forget. I'm damaged goods, just as much as Dilly was."

I objected to his saying that about Dilly, but it wasn't the time to argue with him. As far as confession, or whatever you want to call it, I've found that it doesn't do a thing for me. If I did something wrong, I did it. I'm stuck with it. Out of self-preservation, if nothing else, I try not to hurt people unless I don't have a choice.

"So everybody had sex with her except Everett," I said. "What was he doing while the rest of you were carrying on?"

"I don't know."

"Then, when you guys were finished, you left her. Right?"

"I guess we did."

I wasn't sure I could hide my anger. I knew I had to try, though, if I wanted him to keep talking. "How did you convince Everett to leave? From what you've said about him, he doesn't seem to have been the type to have abandoned her."

"I don't know what he did. He had his own car. When we were through . . . when we . . . It's so ugly, so evil. It hurts to talk about it. Anyway, he wasn't there afterward. Maybe he left when we started doing it."

"Brad said Everett committed suicide. Do you think he did?"

"I don't know that, either. I'd like to think not. Suicide is a sin."

"One of many."

His face twitched. "Yes."

"Let me ask you about something else. I saw Dilly's records from the University of Maryland. There's an item in them about the cops finding her graduation night. It doesn't say anything about rape. She told the campus police that some strangers jumped her and messed her up. She never said a word about any of you. Why do you think she did that?"

McCauley's chest shook as though he couldn't take in enough air to continue to live. "I suppose she was protecting us," he said. "Even after what we did, she protected us."

He stood there, right out on the sidewalk, put his hands over his face, and cried. It was the crying of someone who had abandoned hope. It was painful to hear.

I rarely cry. Maybe that's why other people's tears make me feel awful. I still thought what he'd done was terrible, but I didn't want to know his pain. I said, "Listen, it happened. There's nothing you can do to change it, but there is something that might help."

He clutched at my arms, hurting them. "What is it? Tell me."

After I pried myself loose, I said, "Go to the police if you want to make amends. Let them hear what you told me. It might help them figure out what happened to Dilly and why."

Now he was clutching at his own arms. "I can't do that. I can't repeat things about my friends, not without their permission."

I shook my head. "I'm not so sure you should ask for it."

"Then I can't do it. I'll just have to bear this cross until I die."

He wasn't even thirty. That was a lot of bearing. I said, "Okay. Then make amends in some other way."

"What other way?"

"I don't know, but I'll think about it."

"I could tell her brother and ask him to forgive me."

"No," I said, "I don't think you should do that. He might feel obligated to kill you."

"Then there's nothing I can do."

"Sure, there is." I tried to sound upbeat. "I think the best thing you can do is help other young women in some way. Give them money or counsel them. Pray with them. Whatever you come up with. Dilly would have liked that."

"Do you think so? I mean, do you think that would make me feel better?"

"Yes, I do—unless you killed Dilly. If you did, nothing is going to help you feel better unless you make a full confession to the police."

At least he stopped sobbing, although tears continued to slide down his cheeks. "How could you . . . how could you think I did that? Even my career isn't worth a person's life. I'm sure we all feel the same way."

"I don't believe so," I said. "She didn't kill herself."

CHAPTER
21

My meeting with Bob McCauley left me feeling low. To lift my spirits, I went to the Athletic Club and worked out for an hour and a half. That didn't help as much as I'd expected.

Neither did the envelope I found shoved under my door when I returned from the club. It had in it three tickets for the wrestling matches at the Baltimore Arena that Saturday night, the main bout pitting the Incredible Hulk against someone named Vader. There was also a note identifying a neighbor across the street as the giver and explaining that she couldn't use the tickets because she had to go to New York on business. I wondered if Tom would go with me.

I'd noticed his unmarked was parked outside his house. I barged up his driveway and banged on the door. He took his time about answering.

I shifted from foot to foot until he let me in. My eagerness to see him wasn't because of the tickets, though. I could hardly wait to pass on what I'd heard from Brad and McCauley. Nobody needed to tell me how important it was, at least not after I'd talked to McCauley.

When Tom finally opened the door, I pushed past him, walked into the family room, and shut off the TV. "Why did you do that?" he said, his voice complaining. "I was watching something."

"This is better. I think I know why somebody killed Dilly Friedman."

I proceeded to tell him what Brad and then Bob McCauley had said. He whistled. "I guess we've finally got our motive pinned down."

"Maybe. I'd still like to find out why anyone would wait five years to decide she was a threat."

He said, "I think it's what you came up with before, or maybe it was your boyfriend; I can't remember. Most of these guys have a lot to lose now, more than they did when they graduated. Somebody didn't want to take a chance that Friedman would shoot her mouth off. The next question is, which one of them did it?"

"I don't think it was Bob McCauley," I said. "He's eaten up with guilt as it is."

"Unless the guilt covers more than he let on to you."

That was possible—but I didn't believe it. "I think it was Cohen, Kramer, or Dicky Miller."

"Or all three working together."

Why not? It could have been. I said, "How are we going to find out?"

He shook his head at me. "I've told you and told you—you're not. And I'm not, because it's not my case. I'll pass the word on, though."

He gestured toward one of his chairs. I sat. "Don't look so disappointed, Rachel. You did a good job. We'll go to work on those individuals again because I think we've finally got a handle on this thing, thanks to you."

He was offering me a warm fuzzy to replace what he thought he'd taken from me. He could have saved himself the trouble. I was close, so close. I could feel it; I could smell it. I wasn't about to stop now.

"I appreciate that," I said mildly. He gave me a suspicious look. Not for nothing had he lived next door to me for several years. He knew I didn't cave in, at least not easily.

I said, "How's your needlepoint going?" This had the desired effect of distracting him. I listened patiently to him talking about his hobby, then announced that I needed to go home to do some work myself. I forgot I'd meant to ask him if he was free Saturday night, which was just as well; as I remembered later, Cleome, who would be visiting Saturday, couldn't stand him.

I wasn't lying when I told Tom I needed to go home. I had gotten the okay on two queries I'd sent in to magazines. Now I had to produce. I spent the rest of the day looking up information on my subjects via the Internet. I tried to put the Friedman case out of my mind. It wasn't easy. There had to be a way to trap the killer or killers, only I hadn't figured out what it was.

I wondered if calling them all together would work. Maybe one of them would implicate another, or they'd implicate each other. Then I wondered about how carefully their alibis on the night of Dilly's death had been checked. In any case, these seemed like things the police should handle.

By 8:00 P.M. my eyes were bleary from staring at the screen, and my wrist ached from using the mouse. I shut down the computer and made myself a hot dog for dinner. After that, I decided to go for a drive.

Even though it seemed warmer than it had been earlier in the week, there weren't many people out. Those who weren't in their homes were probably at the local eateries or the movies. I eased into one of the connecting streets and followed it until it ran into a main artery. I didn't see anyone in front of me, and only a few cars passed me going in the opposite direction. I was surprised at how thin the traffic was.

I drove into the center of Fairfield, where the main mall is located. The Mall doesn't close its doors until

9:30, so there was still some activity there. I parked but didn't go in.

I was thinking about Dilly, about which one of her dear friends had killed her. I guess my thoughts distracted me, because I didn't notice that it had become foggy. The wisps of white were pretty, but they wouldn't make driving easy. I left the mall area and headed for home.

The fog got thicker and higher as I drove. I lowered my speed and kept my dims on. When I came to a bridge, I noticed I couldn't see the guardrails. It was as though they'd melted away. I was a competent driver, but still it was a relief to realize that I was almost at my street. Just before I turned into it, I made out the outline of a man walking a large white poodle in the cul-de-sac across the road from mine. Or maybe it was the white mass of the poodle I noticed, and my mind supplied a leash and an owner. Otherwise, there didn't appear to be anyone around.

I pulled into my driveway, then looked over to where Tom kept his car. The space was empty. I wouldn't have minded talking to him again, and not just because I was thinking about the Dilly Friedman case. The fog, isolating me in a seemingly strange place where sight was obscured and sound muffled, made me feel a little lonely.

I started to get out of the car, then remembered that Cleome had left her boom box in my car. I needed to take it into the house. Although it didn't appeal to me at all, I could appreciate that it might seem a great prize to a larcenous teenager. I grabbed it by the handle and pulled it after me.

Gazing up at the sky, I noticed that no stars were visible. Around me there was stillness, as though I were the only thing left alive in the world. Then I heard a whisper of a noise, or thought I did, from across the street. I whirled around but couldn't see anyone. Still, I was pretty sure somebody was nearby.

I continued to sense the presence of another person, but I had yet to see him. Maybe that's what spooked me. I felt the little hairs on the back of my neck stand up. "Who's there?" I called. Nobody answered.

I saw movement from the pavement side of one of the parked cars across the street. The backlight from the houses on that side enabled me to determine that the person was wearing what appeared to be a wide-brimmed hat and some sort of enveloping coat, or maybe a long cape, that disguised his shape.

In fact, the person could have been anybody. With those clothes, it was impossible to tell. The ambiguity made him seem more sinister to me than he otherwise might have.

I called, "Mr. Jones?" That was the name of a man who lived directly across from me. No answer. "Who are you?" I said more loudly.

The person didn't respond.

"What do you want?" I said. I noticed I sounded shriller.

The voice, when it traveled through the fog, was low, indistinct, not determinable as to sex. "I want you, Rachel. Gonna kill you."

I said, "Oh yeah? I'm armed and dangerous."

The person laughed. The sound was creepy.

"Look," I said, stepping a little closer, "this is a joke, right? You're trying to frighten me. I'm not frightened, though. I'm irritated, and I don't have a lot of tolerance. Now, who are you?"

No answer.

I took two more steps forward. So did he.

That's when I came to my senses. I wasn't armed, and I was dangerous only to the extent that the adrenaline pumping through my body made me feel aggressive. But not stupid. I didn't need to confront this person. I needed a safe place where he couldn't get me. I wheeled around and started for my front steps, cursing myself for not taking out my key ring before leaving my car. Even if I couldn't have gotten into the house in time, I could have jabbed the sucker in the face with the keys.

I was right-handed, so I shifted Cleome's boom box to my left hand. The switch made me consciously aware of the box. It must have weighed plenty. If the stalker got close enough and my aim was good, I could maybe knock him out, or at least down my steps. I had to hope I didn't miss because I might not get another chance.

I shifted the box and my fingers touched a knob. That gave me another idea, one I thought had a good chance of working. I turned the radio on as loud as it would go, making the night hideous with the sounds of a heavy-metal band. A harsh male voice sang something about cutting up a two-timing woman.

A door opened two houses away, spreading warm yellow light to the outside. Someone yelled, "Turn that thing down!"

I yelled back, "Oh, yeah? Come and make me."

The shadowy figure turned. I heard a car door open and close and the sound of a motor. The car pulled away from the curb opposite, its lights off. The person who announced he was going to kill me was gone.

Who was it—Jim Cohen, the bus driver Dicky Miller, or maybe Brad Kramer? Surely it wasn't the Reverend McCauley, unless he'd had second thoughts about telling me of his involvement in Dilly's rape.

I shut off the boom box and shoved my hand in my bag. Wouldn't you know it—I found my keys on the first try.

CHAPTER
22

When I got up the next morning, birds were singing, a bushy-tailed squirrel chattered in the tree outside my window, and the sun shone. No fog. No threat. I thought that without too much effort, I could make myself believe that the ugly incident the night before hadn't occurred. Since I prefer reality, even the ugly kind, I didn't make the effort.

I considered whether I wanted to tell Tom what happened, then decided not to. He might tell Jordan, who, given his past responses to my delving into Dilly's murder, would probably say unpleasant things to me. I had no doubt that what happened the night before had to do with Dilly's case.

Thinking about Jordan made me . . . uh . . . think about Jordan. I decided to invite him to go to the wrestling match with me. I couldn't see any reason why Cleome would have anything against him.

I had another thought. Why wait until Saturday to see Jordan? If I could lure him over that night and get him into bed, which I didn't expect to be a problem given his past eagerness, I felt pretty sure my bad mood would evaporate.

"Hi," I said when I got him on the phone. "Do you know who this is?"

I was playing a game of ours. His answer was supposed

to be someone unlikely, if not impossible, like Princess Di or Snow White. It was a good way for us to start off a conversation because it made us laugh. This time, Jordan didn't want to play. He said, "Yeah, it's you, Rachel."

I forged ahead, despite his obvious lack of enthusiasm, and said, "I was wondering if you're available Saturday night. I have three free tickets to the wrestling matches."

"I didn't know you liked wrestling."

"I don't, but Cleome might. I thought you could go with us."

There was a pause. Then Jordan said, "Who's Cleome?"

I couldn't believe I hadn't mentioned her to him, but I guess I hadn't. "She's the little girl from Dilly Friedman's school who visits me some weekends. She'll be here this coming Saturday and part of Sunday."

"When did that arrangement start?"

His tone wasn't particularly pleasant. I said warily, "I don't know. A little while after Dilly was killed, I guess. You'll like Cleome; she's a terrific kid."

There was silence on the other end of the line. Then he said, "I'm not sure I want to go Saturday. I have tentative plans to do something else."

"Don't do it. Say yes to me. We'll have a good time."

I waited. "All right, yes," he said finally.

I could feel myself smiling with relief. "Good. Here's another suggestion: Come over later. I have something for you."

"Oh? What's that?"

"Me."

I'd like to say that he came leaping through my front window before I hung up the phone, but if I did, I'd be lying. In fact, I had to make several sexy suggestions to get him to agree to visit. Fortunately, even very bright men don't always think with their heads.

When Jordan showed up, I was glad I'd gotten in touch with him and even gone so far as to change into the pale blue lounging pajamas Nancy had bought me two Hanukkahs before.

He was dressed in black slacks and a shirt about the same color as my pajamas. He wasn't wearing a tie, and the top two buttons of his shirt were open to reveal the maybe three hairs that grew on his chest. He smelled of Royall Lyme aftershave—I knew what it was because I'd bought it for him for his birthday—and I thought he looked gorgeous. I also got the impression that he was troubled about something.

Not wanting to spoil the mood, which wasn't that good, anyway, I didn't ask him what was wrong. Instead, I put my arms around him and kissed him several times, until he started kissing me. That's when I made my move. Holding his hand, I led him into the bedroom. Then he took over.

I guess we spent more than an hour in bed. Early on, he stopped looking troubled.

Afterward, we showered and dressed, then went into the kitchen. As I think I mentioned before, lovemaking left him feeling hungry. I made him a gargantuan sandwich containing just about everything vegetarian in my refrigerator.

Jordan swallowed a bite of sandwich, then said to me, "Tell me more about Cleome."

I smiled at him, partly because I still felt the afterglow from our time in bed and partly because Cleome was one of my favorite topics. "Jordan, she's a wonderful child. She's tough and street-smart, but there's also an innocence and sweetness about her. We are very fond of each other."

"What do you mean she's tough and street-smart?"

"Well, she'd have to be, wouldn't she, given that she

lives in a high-crime area and has a neglectful mother who's a crack addict? Those things don't matter, though. You'll see that when you and your kids meet her."

Jordan didn't say anything. I waited. Finally, he said, "Why would we want to meet her?"

I felt the muscles in my face tighten. "I told you," I said.

"What you told me was that she doesn't have anything in common with my kids, or me. I ask you again why we'd have any desire to meet her."

"Jordan, you're being a snob."

"Is it snobbish to want to protect my kids from a girl whose mother is a crack addict?"

If I was honest, I'd have to admit it wasn't. On the other hand, I knew Cleome, knew she was wonderful. She was also an important part of my life, one I wasn't willing to get rid of, even for a desirable man. I said, "Why don't you reserve judgment until you meet her?"

"I don't want to meet her, Rachel."

"It's your loss," I said.

"Yeah. Too bad. Let me ask you something else. Are you still messing with that Friedman case?"

I decided to ignore his unattractive choice of words. I said, "I just interviewed someone yesterday who was one of her friends when they all went to the University of Maryland."

"Could this friend have been involved in her death in any way?"

"No, I don't think so, but he definitely was involved in her rape."

Naturally, after saying that I had to tell him everything I'd learned, beginning with what Brad Kramer had told me, and how I'd learned it. His troubled look came back. I said, "What's the matter, Jordan?"

He shrugged.

"Come on, tell me. You're not being fair to me, otherwise."

"I get the impression that you'll do anything to find out what you want to know, Rachel, whether it's the right way to go about it or not."

"Like what?" I said, my voice aggressive.

"Like hiring that hacker."

"I didn't hire him. Nancy did. Besides, he did the job for nothing."

"Don't be so literal. I also don't approve of the way you went after that minister."

"Come on, Jordan, what did you want me to do? Tell him that ruining Dilly's life was okay? That he should just walk away and forget it because she didn't matter? For all I know, he killed her."

"You said before he didn't."

"So? Even if I'm not convinced of it, it's possible. And if he didn't actually kill her, he still helped cause her death. I am as certain as I can be that her rape graduation night was the reason for her murder five years later."

He frowned at me. "How do you know that?"

"I just do," I said. And I did.

"All right. Calm down. The point is, you don't need to be handling any of this. It's what the police get paid for."

"Her brother asked me to. I promised I would." That wasn't exactly true. First and foremost, he'd asked me to write an article about her. If he'd known me, however, he would have realized that I wouldn't stop with that.

Jordan said, "Still . . ."

"There isn't any still. I get the feeling you think I'm immoral. But keeping my promise to Benny Friedman isn't immoral, just the opposite."

Jordan got out of his chair and came over to me. He put a hand on either side of my head, tilting my face so that I had to look at him. "It isn't just a question of morality. Tell me that the only reason you're doing this is because of Benny. Tell me that you don't get a thrill out of this."

I didn't say anything.

"You know, Rachel, the rabbis say that Jews aren't allowed to hunt because hunting doesn't involve a merciful way to kill. Tell me you're not a hunter of people."

What could I say? I knew I was a hunter and that I loved the sport. I said, "What's so wrong about the way I am? You have friends who go out and shoot deer every fall, but you don't say anything to them. Why do you object so strongly to what I'm doing?"

"Maybe because I don't wonder if they'll make a good mother. And maybe I don't wonder if they'll manage to survive long enough to help me raise my children."

He did care about me. That was the first thing I thought. There wasn't any second. I didn't know what to do. If he was seriously considering asking me to marry him and help him bring up his kids, I couldn't blame him for his concerns. At the same time, I knew I couldn't tell him I'd quit trying to learn who had killed Dilly and why. I was too close.

And I certainly wasn't going to give up Cleome.

All of that was in addition to not knowing if I'd even want to take a chance on marrying again. In my eyes, two failures were a humiliation. Three meant I was a damn fool who never learned a thing.

"Look," I said, "you may not realize it, but one of the reasons you like me is that I'm wilder than you are. I bring something to our relationship that you find missing in yourself."

"Thank you, Sigmund. And so what? I was already married to a woman wilder than I am. It didn't work. She divorced me and got herself murdered. Remember?"

"What are you saying, Jordan?"

"I don't know what I'm saying. I'm crazy about you, Rachel, but . . ."

The phone rang just then. If I'd known better, I wouldn't have answered it, but, of course, I didn't know better.

I said hello, but what I got back wasn't anything I could have expected. I heard sounds. They were the sounds of two people having sex. They were the sounds Jordan and I had made just awhile ago.

I guess my mouth dropped open. Jordan said, "What is it? Is something wrong with my kids?"

I shook my head.

"Tell me," he said.

I didn't answer him.

He sped out of the room and came back a moment later holding my portable phone. Now we were both listening. What we heard was my voice asking Jordan what was wrong and his telling me that I shouldn't have gotten a hacker. Etcetera. Etcetera. Word for word.

The conversation ended. The phone went dead.

"I don't understand," I said, feeling violated. "Does that mean my place is bugged? Why would anyone go to that trouble? I don't know state secrets."

Without being aware, I was still gripping the receiver. Jordan took the phone from me and put it back on the cradle.

I said, "Where the hell are the bugs? We've got to find them. I'll look out here and you look in the bedroom."

While Jordan stood there, I took the phone apart, felt under tables, all the stuff I'd seen people do in spy movies. I didn't find anything.

I said, "If you're not going to check the bedroom, why don't you at least help me in here?"

Jordan put his hand on my shoulder. "Let me tell you about the article I read recently on the newer clandestine methods of getting information. One of the things described was a microphone that can pick up conversations from outside a house. No need to break in. No need to plant bugs. These conversations can be taped so they can be played back later, like over the phone."

"Is that what you think this is?"

"It's possible."

This didn't make sense to me. "Even if that's true, why would the person who'd done that want me to know about it?"

"I was wondering that myself, Rachel. I only came up with one explanation that makes sense. Someone is trying to intimidate you, and it's because you persist in meddling in the Dilly Friedman case. Someone wants to scare you, show you how vulnerable you are, so you'll stop what you're doing."

A rat and two mutilated dolls hadn't made me stop. Neither had a voice in the fog. The tape, though it threw me off balance more than the other things, also wouldn't do it. "I haven't quit yet," I said, "and I won't. I'm nearly there. I can feel it."

"Then I guess the other person won't stop. What's next, Rachel? A bomb thrown at your door? A little fire set in your shrubbery?"

"I don't have any shrubbery. You've seen my backyard."

My flippancy seemed to infuriate him more than anything else that evening. "I'm going home," he said.

"How about Saturday night? Are we still on for that?"

For the first time since I'd met him, he raised his voice to me. "No, we're not on for Saturday night. No, I don't want your Cleome to meet my children. No, I'm not attracted to wild women. Now, let me leave before I say something I can't take back. And lock your damn door after I go out."

I said, "If you change your mind about the wrestling matches, let me know."

"When Hell freezes over."

"Does that mean I should give the third ticket to someone else?" I said.

CHAPTER
23

When the phone rang later, I rushed to get it. Maybe Jordan had changed his mind about the wrestling match. Maybe he'd changed his mind about me.

"Hi, Tom," I said unenthusiastically when I recognized my neighbor's voice.

"Don't sound so thrilled to hear from me."

"Okay."

"Hey, if you don't want to talk to me, I can hang up and not tell you what I found out just recently about Dilly Friedman."

"Very cute. You know you have to tell me or be prepared to move."

"Okay, I'll do it while you're driving me to work."

He explained then that his unmarked was being fixed and he hadn't been given another yet. According to him, the cops' cars were always breaking down. "It's my civic duty," I said. "You can count on me."

About ten minutes later, he was in the car, and I was heading for the station in Ellicott City. "Tell me," I said before he even got his seat belt on.

He twisted his body toward me slightly so that he could see my face. "When you told me Dilly was raped graduation night, I passed the information along. The detective on her case got authorization to request her medical records for that time from her doctor and local hospitals."

So, my asking questions had been of help. I smiled, pleased with myself.

Tom said, "He didn't find anything pertinent."

"Oh."

"If she went for treatment after her rape, it didn't show up in our sources. Now we realize she must not have gone."

This was a leap. "Why do you say that?"

He looked out the window. Cars were racing past us, breaking the speed limit by at least twenty miles per hour or more. I figured this obvious flouting of the law must be bothering him. He turned back to me. "Can't you go any faster?"

"That would be illegal. Talk."

"Someday I'm going to get rid of you. I know lots of ways to do it without getting caught."

"Talk," I said again.

"It's like this. A few nights ago, one of the officers was in a bar on Route Forty." He mentioned the place, which I knew from past reports of his was a cop hangout. "He met a woman named Leslie at this bar. He said she was a nice woman even if she was kind of drunk. When he told her he was a cop, she asked him if we'd found out who killed that blond schoolteacher who lived in Fairfield. Those were her words—'that blond schoolteacher.' He figured she was talking about Friedman.

"He asked her why she wanted to know. She said she was sure she'd met Dilly once, only under a different name, which she couldn't remember now. She said she sees a lot of people, but she hadn't forgotten Dilly because she was so brave and pleasant. Leslie said she was shocked when she saw Dilly's picture in the paper."

I turned my head toward him. "Leslie, huh? You were the cop, weren't you?"

"You know, I don't even like you. Stop the car. I'll hitch the rest of the way."

"That's illegal, too. I can't let you do it. Tell me why she thought Dilly was brave. That's not something people usually go around saying."

I tried not to look smug when he dropped the pretense and said, "That's what I thought. I kept asking her about it, but she wouldn't explain what she meant."

"Is that all of it?" I was disappointed.

"No, that's not all. We kept talking. She had a few more drinks. . . ."

"Which you paid for."

"Yeah."

"You deliberately got her drunk so she would open up more, didn't you?"

He looked over my head. "She was drunk when I met her."

"Drunker, then."

"I refuse to answer, and even if I did, it was for a good cause. Also, I drove her home when the place closed. I wouldn't let her take her car."

"You're such an upstanding citizen. Tell me what you found out."

"I learned what Leslie does. She's a nurse at an abortion clinic. Naturally, being the shrewd guy I am, I put two and two together."

"And you came up with the idea that Dilly had an abortion."

"That's right. And when I kept questioning Leslie, she finally admitted Dilly had one at the clinic where Leslie worked at the time. Did I tell you she was drunk?"

I was leaning so far toward him, I was practically in his lap. Tom pushed me back. I said, "Did you find out when Dilly had it?"

"In July, five years ago."

I said, "Dilly graduated in June."

"Yeah."

"One of those SOBs must have made her pregnant."

"Right."

"She could have found out which one if she'd wanted to."

"But, apparently, she didn't and just went ahead and had the abortion."

I wanted to yell at him for saying "just." Even though I'd never been in the position of having an unwanted pregnancy, I couldn't imagine having a pregnancy I didn't want given my barrenness. I was sure a woman having an abortion went through a physical and mental ordeal even when she desired the procedure.

I said, "Do you imagine after all this time she decided to tell the Six-Pack guys what they'd done to her?"

"Could be. From what I've heard, women sometimes get strong feelings about their abortions years after they've had them. Maybe when it was over, she felt she shouldn't have done it. Maybe she brooded about it all that time until she couldn't keep quiet about it anymore."

"That's possible, I guess."

"And maybe she went to each of them and said she wanted money to keep her mouth shut."

"I don't think so."

"Look, Rachel, just because you liked her doesn't mean she wasn't capable of it. If they were afraid of the rape getting out, they might have been that much more afraid if she said one of them made her pregnant and she had to have an abortion. Even if she wasn't asking for hush money, they wouldn't want anyone to know. Can you imagine how Mr. Hunt might react if people said things about his daughter's future husband? Or Jim Cohen's constituents? Dilly

Friedman stood for trouble. Somebody didn't want trouble."

But which one of those guys was it? For reasons I needn't explain, I was betting on Brad Kramer. How could I get the proof, though? And what might he try to do to me if he caught on?

CHAPTER
24

To say that I had a lot on my mind at that time would be an understatement. It wasn't just Dilly's unsolved murder. It was Jordan, too. If it hadn't been for the fact that it was Saturday and Cleome was visiting me, I would have been really in the dumps about him. She cheered me up. I fussed over her, trying to get her to devour the contents of my refrigerator. I guess that's how I show caring, though I'd never been aware of the tendency until I met her.

"How about an orange," I said, "or some applesauce. You need to eat fruit."

"Don't want no more. Appreciate it, but I don't." She gave me a sweet smile, dimples indenting her cheeks, then closed her lips as though I'd force feed her if she didn't. That was probably a wise move; otherwise, I might have tried.

She got up from the table. As soon as she'd arrived at the house, she'd changed into one of the outfits Nancy had bought her—a blue-white-and-red-striped top with red shorts. She looked good. "I like you in those colors," I said.

"Uh-huh. They'd be nice for you, too." There wasn't any disparagement in her tone, but the careful lack of expression on her face told me she didn't think much of my cutoffs and huge gray polo shirt that had printed on it WHEREVER THEY BURN BOOKS THEY WILL ALSO, IN THE

END, BURN HUMAN BEINGS. Generally, I don't wear clothes that make people want to read my chest, but that was a quote I felt people needed to see. Still, I promised myself I'd try to dress better if that was important to Cleome, but I wasn't sure I could be trusted. It was so easy just to throw something on.

"What are we doing today?" Cleome asked as she stretched like a cat. "Anything?"

I thought I'd keep the information about the wrestling match a secret until later. I didn't want her to get too excited, not that she'd shown much evidence of being excitable. Anyway, I always tried to find something "educational" for us to do. I wanted to feed her mind as well as her body. "How would you like to go to the Walters Art Gallery?"

"I already been there. Miss Shelley took us."

"Who's that?" I said, hoping I didn't sound as jealous as I felt.

"One of my teachers."

I tried to hide my disappointment at the ruination of my plan. "Well, maybe . . ." I don't remember what I was going to suggest next, but it didn't matter. The phone rang, and I answered it. The person on the other end was the Reverend McCauley. "Just a minute," I said, then waved Cleome back to a chair.

"How are you doing?" I said into the phone.

"Just fine." To my surprise, he sounded happy. I wondered if maybe he was manic-depressive, and I'd caught him last time in a depressive stage. "I think you saved my life."

"Me? How did I do that?"

"Remember you suggested I find someone I could confess to?"

"I thought you were going to forget about that and do good deeds instead."

"I couldn't forget about it. I knew I could never be at peace if I didn't unburden myself and ask for absolution."

"So you went to the police," I said hopefully.

"Oh no, but I found somebody who had the right to listen and I told all. It worked, too. Now I'm okay. I can go on with my ministry and my life."

"Whom did you find?" I hoped it hadn't been Dilly's brother. I figured he had enough to contend with.

"The person I told asked me to keep it a secret. That's fine; the important thing is I feel as though I've been given a second chance."

"I'm glad," I said, and I was. Even if I had told him I couldn't forgive him, I knew it didn't help Dilly to have him suffer.

"I want to ask you a favor," McCauley said. "I'd like you to visit me at the parsonage today, I want to make lunch for you to compensate for rushing you through our meal at The Crab. Please say yes."

"I don't know," I said.

"Oh, God. You're afraid of me, aren't you? You think I'll rape you."

"That's ridiculous," I said, and I meant it. I couldn't imagine him committing rape ever again. "It's just that I have my friend visiting."

"Bring him along."

"It's a little girl."

"Wonderful. I'd love to meet her. After lunch, I'll show you both my church. It's right next door."

Well, why not? We didn't have anything else pinned down. I said okay and copied the directions he gave me.

I wasn't sure how Cleome would react to the invitation, but when I told her, she said, "That's better than a museum, I guess."

I decided I needed to make myself more presentable

for the occasion. It wasn't every day I got to eat at a parsonage. Actually, up until now, it hadn't been any day. I put on a lavender cotton suit I'd bought about two years before for some now-forgotten occasion, gold hoops, and sandals. I debated first whether I should wear hose. I ruled against it. I wasn't going to Windsor Castle.

We followed the same route I'd taken last time to get to The Crab. Cleome was as little impressed with Purvis as I'd been. I think Fairfield had spoiled her.

Bob McCauley's church and parsonage were on a side street I hadn't gone down before. They were of brown brick, like practically everything else in the town. Both were pseudo-Gothic, not my favorite style of architecture.

I rang the doorbell of the parsonage and waited. McCauley didn't come.

I rang again. Nothing. Then Cleome and I went over to the church. Its arched double doors were unlocked, so I figured Bob had to be inside. Gone were the days when churches and synagogues were left open all the time. There were too many thieves around. We went in.

The interior of the church was dark, gloomy. I think it would have been like that even if all the lights had been turned on, but they weren't. The floor was uncarpeted and the pews plain, dark wood. The main body of the church had a high, vaulted ceiling and stained-glass windows showing scriptural scenes. I recognized Adam, Eve, and the snake in the garden and Abraham wielding a knife so he could sacrifice Isaac. The altar was more elaborate, which, in my opinion, worked against it.

Cleome said, "This don't look like my church. It's too big and dark. I don't like it here."

Neither did I. I called Bob's name, but no one answered. Then Cleome and I started going through the various rooms. The place was empty.

"What do we do now?" she asked.

"We go back to the parsonage and try again. I can't believe he'd invite us to lunch and then not be here."

"Maybe he had an emergency. Maybe somebody died. Maybe he's dead."

"Thanks, kid. Look, let's just go over there."

Back at the parsonage, I rang the bell again. Still no answer. I hit the door with the knocker several times, then waited. Nobody came to let us in. Finally, I turned the fat brass knob. The door opened.

The inside of the parsonage, as far as I could see from the entry, was paneled in dark wood and almost as dim as the church. Only the red-and-green chintz curtains at the living-room windows and the flowered pillows on the brown sofas added a little color. The other rooms we walked through weren't any livelier.

Finally, we came to the kitchen. All the sunlight that was missing in the rest of the first floor seemed to have collected there, mostly due, I think, to the three large French doors that allowed us to take in the garden beyond. One of the doors stood open. It brought in a refreshing breeze and the smell of growing herbs.

The kitchen itself was white—walls, appliances, big table, and chairs. Even the floor was white. The whiteness was a relief after all the brown.

Bob McCauley wasn't in the kitchen, so we walked into the pantry. That was where we found him. He was lying on the floor, on his stomach. There were big, bloody wounds on the back of his head matting down his fair hair. He'd been bludgeoned twice. Blood had run onto his neck and the back of his shirt.

The injury reminded me of the doll someone had left outside of my house. Worse, it reminded me of what had happened to Dilly.

McCauley's right arm was flung out. Next to it was a bowl of egg salad lying on its side. He must have been mixing the salad when he was attacked. A plastic bag and a rope lay near the bowl. Maybe when I knocked at the parsonage door, I'd scared the murderer off before he could use them.

"He's dead, ain't he." Cleome's intonation made it a statement rather than a question.

I said, "Get behind me. Don't look."

"I bet I've seen more dead bodies than you. You don't even watch TV."

"I don't care," I said. "I don't want you in here, looking at him. Why don't you call nine-one-one?"

"Will the police come? Ain't going to call no—"

I said, "You call nine-one-one right now."

She seemed surprised by my tone of voice, but she did what I said.

I knew I had to be careful, that I couldn't do anything to contaminate the crime scene. Still, I needed to know if Bob was still alive. He didn't appear to be—he had that glazed look in his eyes that dead people have—but I kept hoping he was.

"Bob," I said, bending over him. "Can you hear me?"

His eyes opened wider, and he moaned. Emotions—fear, elation—surged through me, but I kept them in check. "Tell me who did this," I said.

A hint of a smile touched his lips. "Doesn't matter."

"It does. Please, tell me."

"Better . . ."

"What?"

"Better is end than beginning."

"Bob, you've got to tell me. Please."

"Soul saved from death."

I didn't want to argue with a seriously hurt man, but I

felt compelled to find out who'd done this. Instead, the reverend was using his little store of energy to quote from the Bible.

"Was it Jim Cohen? How about Dicky Miller?"

I didn't finish the list. I heard Bob sigh. Then he turned his head. It was obvious even to a nonmedical person like me that he was gone.

At least he got to confess and died at peace, I thought.

Then I had another idea. It was possible he'd been killed because of that confession, and according to him, I was the one who got him to make it. Only the arrival of an ambulance and two police officers kept me from sinking to the floor in despair. "Get out of there," one of the cops yelled at me, and I walked away from the pantry, fighting off the tears.

"Were you the individual who called?" the taller of the two officers asked. I shook my head and pointed to Cleome, who had come back into the kitchen. The guy looked from one to the other of us. "What were you doing here?"

When I got through explaining, he said he'd want a statement from both of us. "Fine," I said, "but just let me phone my next-door neighbor, Tom Brant. He's a policeman in Howard County, and he's working on a case that involved the dead man." Actually, I hadn't forgotten that Tom wasn't on the case, except peripherally, but I couldn't remember the name of the detective in charge. I just didn't want to go through a long explanation.

The cop gave me his cellular phone, then stood there while I called. "It's Rachel," I said when Tom got on the line. "I'm at the Reverend McCauley's house. You know, he was one of the Six-Pack. Somebody murdered him, and my friend and I found the body."

"Don't touch anything. I'll put out a call for some officers. What's the address?"

"I already notified the cops. One of them is standing next to me. Would you like to talk to him?"

"Hand him the phone."

When the guy got off the phone, he said, "Brant will be here soon." I felt better, though not by much.

A short while later, a number of other people arrived, including a woman carrying a couple of cameras. There was also a pair of detectives from the homicide squad. One took me into another room to get my statement. The other went off with Cleome. How I wished I could have spared her all this.

Then Tom showed up. I wanted to run to him, but he barely looked at me. Instead, he went somewhere with one of the detectives. When he finally came back to me, I bombarded him with questions.

"Just a minute," he said. "Give me a chance to breathe. Okay, here's what I know. McCauley had two head wounds. They killed him. I guess you saw the bag and the rope, huh? It looks like the same M.O. as in the Friedman case."

"I knew it," I said, but not triumphantly. "At least that leaves out her brother. There's no reason to think he killed Dilly."

Tom was curt. "He wasn't a suspect. Did you think he was?"

I told Tom about my conversations with McCauley. "I was afraid he'd confess to Benny Friedman and Friedman would kill him."

"I would have," Tom said, "but I don't think that's the way it went down."

"Tom, it's got to be one of the Six-Pack."

"Why would the reverend confess to someone who already knew what had happened?"

I said, "I thought of that. I think *confess* isn't the right word. I believe he needed to share with someone how bad he felt about what he'd done and have that person tell him it wasn't his fault."

Tom gave me the disillusioned cop smile. "It didn't work out the way he hoped, did it?"

"And yet he seemed satisfied when he died. I know that because I saw him then." I sniffed, once again wanting to cry but not letting myself.

That's when Cleome came in. She rushed over, glared at Tom as though he were responsible for my state, and hugged me.

"Who's that?" he said, scowling at her. I could tell they weren't going to be friends, ever. I hadn't thought I could feel worse, but I did.

CHAPTER
25

Cleome and I decided to pass up the wrestling match that evening. After seeing Bob McCauley die, we couldn't bear to watch anything violent, even when the violence was obviously scripted. We took the tickets to one of the low-cost housing units in Fairfield and asked the rental office clerk to give them away. She seemed delighted.

We kind of bummed around after that. I knew Cleome wasn't feeling happy because she took off her new clothes, put on one of my heavy old housecoats, and kind of hunkered down. I had the feeling she wanted to suck her thumb but wouldn't let herself.

I finally got her to talk about her feelings a little. "Can't hardly believe it," she said. "And him being a preacher. Ain't nobody and no place safe, is there, Miss Rachel?"

"Looks that way." I felt guilty. Here was this kid from a violent neighborhood, and what had I done? I'd gotten her involved in the worst type of violence there is—murder.

The next morning, I drove her home. We didn't talk much, and I felt a kind of relief when we said good-bye. I think she did, too.

My mood lifted somewhat as I drove back to my house. It was a beautiful day, a day when people should have been pleased with everything. The sky was bright blue and practically cloudless, a rare occurrence in this generally overcast area. The temperature was in the high sixties but felt warmer because there was hardly any wind. If I ignored the man-made structures and concentrated on the trees and spring flowers, things were about as nice as they get around here, which wasn't bad.

Despite the great weather, I didn't linger outside when I got home. I had a lot to think about, like who murdered Bob McCauley and why.

My thoughts were interrupted by the ringing of the doorbell. I looked through my peephole and saw Jim Cohen. I opened the door but kept the chain on. "Hi," I said to soften what came next. "What do you want?"

"Let me in, Rachel. I heard about Bob McCauley on the news. I need to tell you something."

I didn't trust him. I didn't trust any of the remaining members of the dwindling Six-Pack. I eyed him for a few moments. He didn't look any more or less nervous to me than a guy should whose old buddy had just been murdered. I released the chain and allowed him to step past me. Before I could close the door again, though, Brad Kramer and Dicky Miller pushed in after him.

"What is this?" I said as Miller shut my door.

He said, "Don't freak. We just want to talk to you."

He looked his usual lowlife self—black leather vest over bare skin, black pants and boots, and lots of silver jewelry. The other two were dressed casually but more conventionally, in knit pullover shirts and slacks. "Okay, talk," I said, as I continued to stand by the door.

Brad's smile was unpleasant. "The little lady doesn't trust us," he said. "She wants to be able to get out fast if we pull any rough stuff."

Jim Cohen said, "Can we go in the living room? We really need to talk to you."

I didn't see too many choices at this point. I knew Tom wasn't home. At least the portable phone was in the living room. "Come on," I said.

When they sat down, Cohen looked around and said, "Nice place." Brad snickered, but who cared? I took a corner of the couch. "Talk," I said.

Jim said, "There's a killer loose out there."

I shook my head. "I think he's in here. Any of you want to fess up?"

Unless Jim was a darn good actor, he was genuinely shocked. "Are you out of your mind? Somebody is after us. First Dilly was killed, and then Bob. If we don't stop this maniac, one of us will be next."

"Okay, I'll say it to you again—which of you is the maniac?"

He said, "You think one of us killed them?"

"Of course I do. Who else could it be? You don't have to worry, though. The police will arrest the last of you left alive."

Brad Kramer half rose from his chair. "You've got a real smart mouth. I'd like to . . ."

"Think hard," I said. "You've already left a dead rat on my doorstep."

His expression became indignant. "That wasn't my idea."

"How about the doll with pins stuck in her heart, and the one with fake blood dripping from her head and neck? Oh, you guys are cute."

Kramer was grinning. "You forgot one—taping your sex orgy with your boyfriend. I did that. I'll admit to it." He laughed. "You're a hot number, Rachel, a lot hotter than you look."

I said, "You're not."

The other two laughed; he didn't. Jim said, "Okay, we did those things. We were trying to scare you a little, to get you to stop prying. We didn't hurt you, though."

"What about sneaking around across the street from me that night in the fog, saying you were going to kill me? Which of you psychopaths is responsible for that?"

I got three blank stares. Miller said, "What are you talking about? Nobody snuck around, except to throw the rat and all."

He was probably lying. But why lie about that incident? Maybe the one who pulled it off had different intentions. Maybe he did mean to kill me. Which one was it? Eenie, meenie, minee, moe . . .

I asked, "What do you want now?"

Jim said, "We want you to stop asking questions. Leave everything alone. Then, maybe, this stuff will stop."

"Why did it start?"

He said, "We don't know. But whatever's going on, you're the catalyst. The police weren't even interested in us at first. Now they are. And it's your fault."

"Dilly wasn't killed because of me."

I got the blank stares again. I said, "Let me tell you what I know. I know what you did to Dilly graduation night because Brad told me."

"You mean what I said about leaving her at the university?"

"That's not all you said, was it, Brad? You told me four of you had sex with her."

Miller looked angry. "Why did you tell her that?"

"Don't say you're ashamed of what you did. No, now I remember. You're not ashamed because she asked for it by falling on the floor. You're just afraid some people might not understand that it was all her fault."

"Lay off," Brad said.

I stared into his eyes. "I repeated to Bob McCauley what you said, and he told me you guys raped her."

"He said that?"

"Yes, he did. He told me Dilly cried and asked you all to stop. That's rape in my book. The police would think so, too. What I want to know is which of you charming rapists murdered her."

Cohen said, "You're nuts. Why would we do that?"

Their attempts to make me think they were innocent really got on my nerves. What would they say if I told them Dilly had had an abortion? Would they lie even more? I decided not to mention it. I said, "Let's try to guess. We'll start with you, Jim. How would the fine citizens of Howard County react if they knew you'd raped a defenseless female and caused one of your pals to kill himself? You couldn't get elected for skunk catcher."

"Just a minute. . . ."

"And you, Brad. Mr. Hunt wouldn't let you sweep his warehouse, let alone get near his precious daughter, if he knew what you'd done. I'd say you had plenty of reason to kill Dilly. As long as there was a chance she'd talk, both of you were in jeopardy. All three of you were."

"Yeah?" Miller said. "Then who killed McCauley, and why? That's what's got me worried."

"Probably the same one who killed Dilly, and for the same reason. McCauley was filled with guilt. He wanted to confess, put his transgressions on the table. Unlike you boys, he never got over what he did."

Miller said, "So?"

"So he found someone to confess his feelings to."

Miller looked shocked. "Are you saying a priest murdered him?"

"No, I think one of you did it. Why would anyone else?"

Kramer didn't even bother to look insulted. "That's the question, isn't it?" he asked.

Jim Cohen's voice was urgent. "Which one of us?"

I stood and moved toward the window, wanting to put distance between me and them. "The one he confessed to, of course. Or was it to the three of you?"

"Why would he confess to us? We already knew—not that I'm admitting we raped her," Jim said.

"I think he believed that if he spoke to one or all of you, you'd convince him that what had happened wasn't so bad. Instead, he was murdered."

Miller said, "You're crazy if you think I killed McCauley."

"And Dilly," I said, "unless two killers are running around."

Jim slumped in his chair. He put his head in his hands. His voice muffled, he said, "I didn't do it."

"If that's true, it's a choice between Kramer and Miller. Well, men, which of you knocked off two of your old college chums? And do you have plans to do in the other two?"

Miller said, "You bitch!"

Brad Kramer's face was pale and twisted, as though he had a terrible bellyache. "I didn't murder anyone. I'd never do that. I'm a businessman."

That was a non sequitur if I'd ever heard one, but I let it pass. "Somebody did," I said.

They looked at me, then at one another. None of them had anything to say.

"Listen," I said, "this isn't working. You're wasting my time. You try to figure it out."

Jim Cohen smoothed his blond hair back with a sweep of one hand. He seemed as though he was about to make a speech, but what he said was, "You're right. That's what we need to do."

Brad Kramer said, "I'm not going to do it. This is ridiculous."

I moved closer to the three of them. "I vote for him as the number one suspect."

I should have stayed where I was. He was on me almost faster than I could track him. He put his hands on my arms and started shaking me. It wasn't fun. I could feel the stress to my neck. I said, "Let go of me, sucker."

The other two grabbed him. He took his hands off me and started swinging at them. They pushed him into a chair and told him to stay there.

I wasn't so sure he would. He was back to glaring at me. I said, "Look, guys, if you can't handle him, I'm going to call Animal Control to come get him."

This didn't go down well with Kramer, either, but political Jim finally calmed him. Then, as soon as I could, I hustled them out. I'd had enough networking for one day.

CHAPTER
26

I woke up in the middle of the night. Some kind of whistle or alarm was going. At first, I merely felt irritation because I don't like noise. Then I realized what I was hearing was a smoke alarm. I turned on a light, got into a robe and slippers, fast, and started hunting for the reason for the sound.

I could smell smoke, but I couldn't see anything—not until I looked out the door. Billows of it were coming from the extreme left side of the house. That's where my garage was.

I grabbed the portable phone and ran outside. It was my garage going up, all right. The smoke was thick. Gold-and-red flames shot out of the walls and through holes in the roof. I called 911.

My car was parked in the driveway. I never put it inside. I moved it to get it out of the way of the fire trucks I could hear racing up one of the nearby main streets.

I'd used the garage as a repository for yard tools I bought but never did anything with and extra chairs and things that I didn't have a place for but didn't want to get rid of. That included maybe a thousand books. Oh, damn, I thought. My books.

When a Torah scroll, containing the five books of Moses, is worn out, Jews don't throw it away. They bury it as though it were a revered human being. I've never done that with a book, but I understand the feeling. I really *love* the written word. It's hard for me to get rid of a book. And I've actually thrown only one away in my whole life, because it was so sadistic I couldn't even bear to pass it on to anyone else. Now boxes and boxes of my books had gone up in flames.

I realized Tom was standing next to me. I asked him how this had happened. He went off to talk to a fireman, then came back. "It looks like arson," he said.

Arson.

I don't know how long I stood there staring at what was left of the fire. The loss of the garage wasn't that bad. The whole thing would have to come down, of course. Thank heavens for insurance, I thought. Thank heavens for—nothing. I decided I was sick of being brave and martyrlike; it wasn't my style. "Damn," I said. "Damn and damn. Also f—"

I didn't get to finish the word. Tom jerked my arm, then propelled me to his house. I spent what was left of the night there, lying on his lumpy couch, because even though my home itself wasn't damaged, the rooms smelled scorched. I don't think I slept, but it wasn't the couch that kept me awake. I probably could have used a few hugs and back pats, only I was afraid to ask Tom for them, afraid of what they might lead to. I kept my distance, emotionally as well as physically, not wanting to ruin a good friendship. When the morning came, I quietly opened his front door and walked outside.

The day was beautiful. The sun was shining, the sky was a gorgeous medium blue, the air smelled sweet with the odors of flowers and grasses, except around my house, which still stank of burned things.

I hadn't gotten a good look at the damage to my garage the night before. It was dark, it was late, and I was too shocked by what happened to take in much. Came the morning, and I did look. What a mess. Thanks to the fire engine equipment, my front yard was ruined. Of course, that was no great loss. What got to me was the charred and soaked paper strewn everywhere—those poor books.

It certainly could have been worse, however, not that I found the thought especially consoling at that point. If I'd kept cans of kerosene and other inflammables around, there might have been an explosion. The whole house could have gone.

Was that what the arsonist had expected to happen?

Suppose I asked Cohen, Kramer, and Miller if they'd done this. Of course, they'd deny it; arson, unlike mutilating dolls, was a serious offense. Would they look innocent the way they had when I'd asked which of them had whispered I should die that night in the fog? Why had they sworn they hadn't done that?

Everybody has thoughts that flit on the outer edges of the mind, that reveal a tantalizing glimpse of an idea but can't quite be grabbed. That's the way it was with me now. Something I needed to understand about Dilly, Bob, and me and our relationship with the Six-Pack survivors was dancing out there, but I couldn't catch it yet. I felt frustrated, certain it was important and that I'd better be successful soon. If only I could think of it.

I hadn't noticed when Tom came outside until he said, "I don't blame you for frowning, babe. But it will be okay. The insurance company will take care of everything. You do have insurance, don't you?"

"Of course. You can't even get a mortgage without it."

"So, don't worry."

He was still in his pajamas, covered now by a ratty tan robe. His hair was combed, but he hadn't shaved. Mr. Virility had a beard that would have sliced off the top layer of my skin if he'd gotten a millimeter closer. I said,

"I'm not worried. I'm angry—and I want to know who did this."

"Right, and when we find out, I'll personally make sure he goes away for a long time. Come back in my house, Rachel. Let's talk about this."

I followed him inside, staying behind him until we got to the kitchen. He stopped in the doorway and waved at me to precede him. The table was set for two. Tom had put orange juice in both glasses and set bagels, cream cheese, and butter on the table. "Sit," he said. "I'll get the coffee."

I looked up at my old friend, grateful for his thoughtfulness. "Knock it off," he said. "Drink your juice."

"Sure."

He took a sip of his, made a face, then said, "What's going on, Rachel? Who would do that to you?"

"Maybe the same person who killed Dilly Friedman and Bob McCauley."

"You really think there's a connection between them and you?"

I leaned an elbow on the table. "You once asked me whom I'd irritated lately, and I had a list. This time, there are only three people on it. They're Cohen, Kramer, and Miller, the ones I've kept after about Dilly."

"Do you think they set fire to your garage?"

"If it was arson, who else?"

"I told you that you should stay out of it."

I looked at him coldly.

He shrugged. "Sorry. So you're saying those three did it to you."

"I'm not sure, Tom, but they admitted harassing me."

I told him about the doll incidents and the voice whispering to me in the fog. Then I informed him about the visit the day before from the remaining Six-Packers, leaving out only the part about Brad Kramer getting physical with me. If I hadn't, Tom might have gone looking for him to rearrange his features. He was protective of females, and for a female friend, there wouldn't be many limits.

When I finished, he said, "You mean you let them in your house?"

I stood. "I'm going home."

"Rachel, I'm sorry. Sit down. Speak. I won't say another word about the idiotic things you've done. I promise."

I can't say I was appeased, but I had to talk this business over with him. If I did, maybe the thought I was trying to dredge up would come within my reach. I said, "One or two or the three of them killed Dilly and Bob."

"Why are you so sure?"

"Who else could it be? In all the time since Dilly was killed, has anyone else emerged as a suspect? No," I answered my own question. "You can't deny they might have a motive, and nobody else she knew seems to."

"You make a good point. I'm going to suggest that the pressure be stepped up on them. I think Jerry should go see them again, starting with Cohen and Kramer. He'll get them to tell him where Miller's hanging out."

"Who's Jerry?"

"The detective assigned to the case."

"Oh. Has he asked them where they were when Bob was murdered?"

Tom's mouth contorted into an I-don't-know expression. "I doubt it. I'll find out and tell you."

I was pleased he wasn't going to try to exclude me again. "I appreciate that," I said, then added, "And they all had the means."

"But we don't have any proof—no eyewitnesses, no forensic evidence tying them to the victims, no rumors, even—at least not concerning Dilly's murder. This isn't a movie, Rachel, where things have to turn out just because that's what the audience wants. As of now, there's not a thing to build a case with. In addition to that, we've got three suspects, not just one. There's nothing clear here."

"So what happens next?"

"We question them, try to break them down, see if we can get one to turn against the others. There isn't anything else."

"Let's just hope it's enough."

CHAPTER
27

Saturday came. I deliberated about whether I should drive up to Baltimore and get Cleome. I still had the feeling—even stronger than before—that something was about to happen. If it did, I didn't want her around. She got so upset, though, when I suggested over the phone that we skip that weekend, I didn't have the heart to insist.

I picked Cleome up about nine and brought her to my house. The weather didn't match my feeling of foreboding. It was a perfect day: warm but with a breeze that carried with it the scent of freshly turned dirt and young grass even in Cleome's blighted neighborhood. As we got closer to Fairfield, the scene got prettier and prettier. So did the aroma, the sweet odors of flowers added to the mix. I almost wished I had contributed by planting a rose bush or something, but I hadn't.

Just before we got to my street, I remembered that Cleome didn't know about my garage being torched. I had to warn her. "There was a little fire at my house," I said without preamble. "It was an accident and only to the garage, so it was nothing."

"I'm glad." She sighed and I saw her hand shake.

When we got home, she barely gave the garage a second look. I was pleased about that. Still, I wasn't dumb enough to think she wasn't concerned about the fire, or that she'd forgotten she'd seen the Reverend McCauley die. That's why when Nancy called and said she wanted to take Cleome to a Disney movie, I agreed.

They left. Nothing happened. I polished an article I'd been working on about a man who ran a lab that raised special strains of mice for research. The article was due two weeks later, so I was in good shape.

The phone rang just as I finished. I wondered which of the three Six-Packers it would be. Instead, my caller was Mrs. Pearl, wanting to visit me. She said, "I have something to show you concerning Dilly's case, dear. It could be important."

"Show me? What is it?" I asked, wondering if she had found the murder weapon or some other incriminating object in the home of one of the Six-Packers.

"Oh no. It won't do any good to talk about it over the phone. You need to see it. I'd like to come over now, if I may." This statement was followed by a girlish giggle.

Maybe this was the "something" I'd been waiting for, the object or piece of information that would solve the puzzle. I hated to turn her down if there was a chance it was. Besides, she seemed so determined to have me see whatever it was, I had a feeling she'd be at my place whether I agreed to it or not. "To be honest," I said, "I don't see how I can get your chair in my house. Maybe I should visit you."

She laughed. "It's a nice day. Why don't we meet in your backyard? You do have one, don't you?"

Even town houses have backyards. Mine, in fact, had a table, a little rusty but bright red where the paint still adhered, and some chairs.

Before I could say yes or no, she said, "I'll be there in about twenty minutes."

As I waited for her, I planned how I would maneuver

her up my drive and then to the rear. When she arrived, I did it just that way, stopping only once to explain why my garage looked so bad. I barely raised a sweat.

As usual, Etta Pearl was dressed as though she were sixteen instead of fiftyish. Make that fourteen. She was wearing a pink dress with ruffles along the front. This outfit was dolled up with a necklace of pink and white crystal beads, and a white blanket covered her useless legs. On her feet, like defiantly waving flags of defeated nations, she wore bright red shoes.

"Tea?" I asked after I pushed her up to the table.

"Actually, I was wondering if we could go inside. The sun does terrible things to the skin," she said, winking conspiratorially as though we were two teenagers talking about the important things in life. "Wrinkles, you know."

I grimaced. "I'd love to invite you in, but I don't think it's possible."

"Of course it is, you silly girl. Look at that big sliding glass door over there that leads into your basement. I could get inside without a bit of trouble."

She was right. It wasn't any trouble. Actually, my basement isn't all that bad looking. A friend of mine left some very nice living-room furniture there about three years ago and still hadn't retrieved it. I had set it up in a seating arrangement, although I never sat in it. I wheeled Mrs. Pearl over next to the coffee table, lit one of the lamps stashed downstairs, and eased onto the pretty rose-colored sofa. The setup was quite cozy.

Naturally, I wanted Etta to get to the subject, but she insisted on chatting for a while. "How is that darling little girl you see on the weekends?" she said.

Had I told her about Cleome? I couldn't remember. I said, "She's fine. She's at the movies with my friend Nancy."

She grinned archly. "Is Nancy the blonde who was flirting with Rabbi Neufeld at Dilly's memorial service?"

"That's the one. Oh, and speaking of Dilly, what was it you wanted to show me?"

"Show you?" She tucked her feet under her blanket. "Did I say I wanted to show you something? I suppose I did. Now what was it?" She felt around in a large pocket that hung from one of the arms of her chair. Her hands came out empty. "I hope I didn't leave it at home. Oh, well."

Was it the vagueness of the "Oh, well" that did it? Who knows what jogs the memory? All of a sudden, I remembered the thing I couldn't think of before. It was something Tom had told me months earlier. He said that most criminals, not being particularly bright, repeated their behavior time after time. They created a pattern; that's how detectives identified their work. A pattern was cutting a rat's throat and leaving the bloodied creature on my doorstep, hanging by the neck a doll that had a picture of my face pasted over its face, stabbing bloody pins into another doll that also had a picture of me over it. Not fitting that pattern was whispering a death threat on a foggy night and setting fire to my garage. Not fitting that pattern meant that possibly someone besides Cohen, Kramer, and Miller was doing things to me.

Who could that be? Mrs. Pearl was the likeliest suspect. No one else was involved. No one else cared about Dilly and Bob and the rest. No one else cared about Everett Pearl.

Everett had to be the key. I couldn't think of another person who would affect Mrs. Pearl strongly enough to make her commit murder.

But the woman couldn't walk. She was in a wheelchair, for God's sake. She might have been able to shoot her victims, but they hadn't been shot. She couldn't have strangled Dilly, hit McCauley, or stood across from my house. If she were the one behind the killings, she had to have had an accomplice. Who could it be? And was he around now? I turned jerkily toward the window. I didn't see anyone lurking outside. Maybe she kept him under her blanket, I thought, wanting to giggle myself.

Nerves. I had nerves. Knock it off, I muttered in an imitation of Tom. You can handle this. What I needed was time, time to figure out how to get her to confess.

Did you ever hear the expression, the idiot in the attic? That's what some book editors call the heroine of a novel who stupidly goes up alone to the attic to investigate a strange noise that is maybe being made by the murderer. I wasn't an idiot, and this place wasn't an attic. It had the possibility of being a trap, though. I went over to the door and fiddled around, making sure the latch was on. If Mrs. Pearl did have an accomplice, I didn't want him pushing his way into my basement and cornering me.

Etta glanced at me curiously. "I like to look out of the window," I said.

She nodded, obviously no longer interested. She said, "I was teasing you before. I do have something to show you." She gave me a coy look. "First, though, I want you to tell me everything you know about Dilly's and Bob's cases."

I lifted my eyebrows at her. "I don't see this as a game, Mrs. Pearl."

Again, the coy look. "No, no, no. If you don't tell, I won't show."

Maybe if I told her, I could get her to reveal something incriminating. Even if I couldn't, I didn't seem to have a choice. I wanted to see what she had. "What I know is this," I said. "Whoever killed Dilly also killed

Bob McCauley. The connection between them is the Six-Pack."

"I think so, too," she said. "But what could it be?"

Here goes, I thought. "I sort of figure it's your son, Everett."

She gave me a shocked look. "My Everett? How could you say that? He was a saint. He'd never kill anyone. Besides, he was dead when they were killed. He is dead." Her voice wasn't girlish anymore, nor was her face. It was flushed, angry; the softness had been replaced by harsh, bitter lines.

This was going to be hard, but I had to do it. "You told me he died of an accidental overdose. Isn't that right?"

"Of course it's right."

"Some people say he committed suicide, Mrs. Pearl."

She pushed forward in her chair, as though she were about to fling herself out of it. Instead, she held on to the arms. "Who said that? Who?"

"Some of the guys in the Six-Pack."

"That's absurd. He wouldn't have done that. He had no reason to. He was talented and happy. He had graduated. He was engaged to Dilly."

I shook my head. "I don't think so, Mrs. Pearl."

Her face got so red I was afraid she was going to have a stroke. "Why don't you think so? Is it because of things those degenerates said about my boy?"

"In a way. Look, I need to know something. I'm sorry this is painful."

"Painful? Why should it be? You are lying, like the rest of them. Just remember, Rachel, those who lie shall perish. The Scriptures say so."

"Listen, Mrs. Pearl, did you know that the guys in the Six-Pack raped Dilly graduation night?"

"Not Everett."

"No, not him."

Her nostrils flared with scorn. "Dilly told me that. Do you think you've surprised me?"

"When did she tell you?"

She shrugged. "About a year before she died. I'm not sure I believed her, but at least she had the decency to say that Everett wasn't involved."

"Did she tell you that he left her as it was about to happen?"

"She told me. That just shows what a good boy he was. He didn't want to be mixed up in anything sordid. As an artist, he was very sensitive."

I said, "Could he have killed himself because he abandoned her to those wolves?"

"Why should he have?"

"Out of shame, Mrs. Pearl, or that sensitivity you mentioned. He didn't protect her. He walked out."

The red had left her face. "You sound like Dilly and that fool McCauley. Everett wouldn't have done that. He was gallant. He left because he could see that Dilly wanted to have sex with them, but he didn't intend to take any part in it."

McCauley, huh? That's it, I thought. You've given yourself away. But I still needed to get a confession.

CHAPTER
28

"Are you saying that Dilly and Bob McCauley told you that Everett left her at the university?"

"Of course they did. They told me a lot of things. I was like a mother to them, especially Dilly."

"When did they talk to you about it?"

"Dilly told me nearly a year ago. I can't remember when Bob talked to me. It was maybe four months ago. Why? Are you trying to say that I killed them? That I'm lying about when I talked to Bob, and I killed him? How could I have managed that? I'm in a wheelchair."

I shot another glance through the window. If she had an assistant in murder, he wasn't out there. "That's a good question, Etta. Why don't you tell me the answer?"

"You've always seemed like such a nice girl. I liked you the minute I met you. I can't understand why you're talking like this to me." The childish voice was back.

"I'm sorry. I'm doing it only because I want to get at the truth."

"I do, too, and I'm telling you, dear, you're wrong. I couldn't kill anyone, or get someone else to."

That's what they all said.

"Besides, even if Everett did walk out and abandon Dilly, as you insist, it's not as bad as what the others did. Why would I have murdered those two for saying it?"

"I don't know. Maybe it was because you couldn't

pretend anymore that Everett OD'd accidentally; he had a reason to commit suicide."

"I can see why you're a writer, Rachel. You have a strong imagination. You're wrong, though. If Everett had killed himself, and it had been over abandoning a girl in jeopardy, I would have been sorry but proud of him for the delicacy of his feelings. I'd never kill Dilly and McCauley for telling me that."

That made sense, damn it. I said, "Maybe it was something else they said that drove you to murder. Did Dilly tell you she had an abortion about two months after she was raped?"

"Yes, she told me, only not until last year. I think she was ashamed of doing it, but I told her it was the right thing. My God, dear, she was only twenty-one, just out of school and without a job. Who could condemn her? I never could. Of course, if she had decided to go through with the pregnancy, I would have helped her raise the baby, just as I helped her by renting her the house so cheaply. I'm a good woman, Rachel, and I felt particularly close to Dilly. Why can't you see that?"

I moved away from the window. Maybe I was wrong. It wasn't just that I couldn't think of a reason why Etta would kill two people. There was the inescapable fact that she was confined to that chair. Yet, I still believed I wasn't wrong.

I caught a wisp of a smile on Etta's face as I looked at her, just before the expression disappeared. It was a triumphant smile. It wasn't the smile of an innocent woman. She believes she's stumped me, I thought. There had to be some way to get to her, to get her so riled up that she'd lose her self-control and blurt out the truth. There was something else I could tell her, but it wasn't anything one said lightly to an unsuspecting mother. Even though it might work, did I have the right to say it?

I decided I didn't have the right not to. Two people had been murdered, and three more were afraid they were going to be. I said, "Did Bob McCauley tell you that Everett was a homosexual, that that's why he didn't join in the orgy? He wasn't being noble. Dilly wasn't his type."

What kind of reaction had I expected? At first, I didn't get any, except that Etta's complexion grew dangerously red again. Then, like an exploding geyser, she burst from her seat and took a few steps toward me. I guess my mouth flew open, and I looked pretty dumb. Why not? In spite of whatever suspicions I'd nurtured, I was shocked.

"What . . . ? How . . . ?" I sounded dumb, too.

Etta raised her hand. There was a gun in it. "You're too athletic to kill with a pipe," she said. "You'd get away from me."

"You murdered them."

"Yes. No one has the right to lie about my son."

"I . . ."

"You want to tear him down, as they did, because you're jealous. You're a nothing, Rachel, a hack writer of hack articles. My son was a genius. That's what's driven you and them to try to demean his image. But I won't let you. I'm going to memorialize him in that scholarship. His name will be remembered forever."

"How long have you been walking?" I said. "Were you ever incapacitated?"

She lowered the hand holding the gun. "I guess there's time to tell you. Why not? You're not going anywhere. I became paralyzed after Everett died. The doctor—you met that fool of a doctor—he said the paralysis was psychological. Such nonsense. It was God's doing because I had failed somehow as a mother. I knew that, and I couldn't get better. Then when Dilly told me about the rape and abortion last year, when I said the baby might have been Everett's and she said about him what you just said, I felt the paralysis going away. The pain was terrible. I almost cried out, but I didn't. I knew that God was telling me it was time to punish her for her scandalous lies. But I couldn't. I hadn't walked for four years, and my legs wouldn't hold me."

I stared at her in horror. "You worked to strengthen them for a year, didn't you, planning all that while to kill Dilly?"

"Of course I did. And it took a year. I was so weak and helpless for a time. Then I wasn't, and I knew I was ready to stop her garbage mouth."

I thought of something. "Did you quit going to the doctor because you feared he'd realize there was strength in your legs?"

"Strength and feeling. Yes."

I said, "You didn't even do this in the heat of anger, which I could maybe understand. You planned it all this time."

She shrugged. "I didn't have any other choice."

"And Bob McCauley?"

"He came to me. He said he wanted to confess, and I would be the perfect person to confess to. Then he told me his sordid lies. I pretended to believe him, and he seemed so relieved."

I shook my head. "I don't think he told you that Everett was gay. He wasn't the type to talk about other people."

Etta said, "He didn't say it at first. I guess I kept badgering him, hoping he'd retract the nasty things he'd already told me. Instead, he finally said that. So, I had to kill him. I'm going to kill you, too, and it's your fault."

"My fault?"

"Yes, I tried to scare you off. One night I stalked you,

but that didn't work. Then I set fire to your garage. That doesn't seem to have worked, either."

So my theory had been right. There wasn't much comfort in it at the moment.

I moved back toward the sliding door. Maybe I could escape before she took a shot at me. Mrs. Pearl waved the gun. "Get away from there."

I needed time, time to think of a plan, time for somebody, maybe, to spot us and stop her, though that wasn't likely. Time was the only possible thing I had working for me. "Listen," I said, "I still don't see how you managed to kill them. Who's in this with you?"

Her laugh was scornful. "No one. Just me. I told you before that people shouldn't think those confined to a wheelchair are helpless."

"But you're not confined to a wheelchair."

A little smile appeared on her face. "I keep forgetting. To answer your question, though, it was easy to kill them because they weren't expecting it. All they had to do was turn their backs on me for a minute, and I hit them. Once they were down, the rest was easy."

She shifted from one foot to the other. The red shoes looked deadly to me now. "I'm getting tired of this. I'm sorry, Rachel."

"One more question," I said. "Did my showing up at McCauley's place stop you from suffocating him?"

She giggled. "It did. It was all right, though. He died anyway."

I thought I heard a sound behind Mrs. Pearl. Without moving my head, I slewed my glance in the direction of the noise. I saw a few dark braids sticking out one side of the water heater, each one closed with a brightly colored clasp. I didn't know how Cleome had managed to get downstairs so quietly. I didn't know why she had thought to come down. I didn't think she would be back from the movies so early. But I was glad and sorry she was there, torn between wanting her help and wishing she were somewhere else, out of harm's way.

The next thing I knew, Cleome had closed the distance between herself and Etta and shoved the wheelchair against the older woman's legs. Mrs. Pearl went to the floor. I screamed at Cleome to move and threw myself on my would-be killer.

Mrs. Pearl raised the gun, then slammed it down, missing my head but hitting my shoulder. I don't know why she didn't try to shoot me with it. Maybe she got confused and thought she was still using a pipe to dispatch her victims. Whatever, the pain was bad. Any inhibitions that might have been restraining me from hitting a woman old enough to be my mother went out the door. I grabbed her hair with one hand and punched her in the nose with the other. I think I broke her nose.

She seemed stunned, but I could see she still had hold of the gun. It was Cleome who got it away from her. I think she did it by biting Mrs. Pearl on the arm.

Mrs. Pearl ignored her, thank goodness. Instead of trying to reach the kid, she hit me on the breast with her fist. That's a very painful place for a woman to be hit, but at least it took my mind off my shoulder.

I pulled away reflexively, then socked her hard again. I can't say she went down, because she was already down, but she stopped struggling and lay there.

"Call nine-one-one," I yelled at Cleome. "Get the police."

This time she didn't argue with me.

CHAPTER

29

The police came and took Mrs. Pearl, her wheelchair, her gun, and her other accoutrements away. I went back upstairs, swearing to myself I'd never go in the basement again. That thought led to another: Why had Cleome gone down there?

As we sprawled on the living-room sofa, each with a cold cream soda in hand, I asked her. "I came back from the movie. I went in your house, but I couldn't find you. I figured you were home, though, because your car was outside."

Was this kid a baby detective or what?

"I went out again and looked in the backyard. You weren't there, but then I saw you in the basement, through the window. Saw that Mrs. Pearl, too, with a gun in her hand."

"So you went in the house again and then snuck down the basement stairs, right?"

"That's right. I did that."

"You were wonderful, Cleome."

"Wasn't nothing."

But it was, and I was deeply touched. It wouldn't have been a good idea to get emotional, however. That would have made Cleome uncomfortable. I stood, put my soda can on the end table, then pulled the kid to her feet. "Come on," I said.

I took Cleome to Friendly's for ice cream sundaes. As I was spooning down some peanut butter cup, I realized something I hadn't before. I said, "You got out of that movie pretty early, didn't you?"

"Yes, ma'am."

"How come?"

She looked at me shyly. "I made Miss Nancy take me home. I told her I was sick, but that wasn't it."

"Then what was it?"

"It was a feeling I had. I knew you were in trouble and needed me. So, I came back. Good thing, too, huh? I helped you."

"You saved my life." I got kind of choked up then, and not from the ice cream. "I love you, Cleome," I said.

"Your sundae is melting."

It was okay. She didn't have to say she loved me. Her behavior told me everything I wanted to know.

After we finished our ice cream, I realized it was dinnertime, so we stayed where we were and ordered tuna fish sandwiches. When we finished, Cleome said, "Guess I wasn't lying. I do feel kind of sick." I paid the bill and we went back to my house.

The phone rang several times that evening, but I let the answering machine take the messages. At some point, the doorbell rang, too. We ignored it. The truth is, we were both exhausted. I think we went to sleep about eight that night.

I listened to the phone messages the next day. One was from Cleome's mom's friend Betty, asking me to call her. I felt guilty and worried when I recognized her name. Maybe something terrible had happened to Cleome's mother, and I had ignored the message until now. When Betty answered the phone, I said, "This is Cleome's friend, Rachel Crowne. Is everything all right at her house?"

"Well, nothing's different. Her mama called and said she wouldn't be coming back till Monday afternoon, so if you are willing to keep Cleome and drive her to school Monday, you can."

Was I willing to win the lottery? I said yes. I may have said it twice. Things were looking good for me, and I was feeling very cheerful.

When I told Cleome, she seemed downcast at first, I guess because of her mom's not bothering to come home, but she cheered up fast, especially when I promised to take her to Friendly's again later for another sundae. She stayed in a good mood, in fact, until Tom came over. Then she deflated. She still wasn't ready to accept a cop as a decent, trustworthy human being.

Tom ignored her and talked to me. "You had a real ordeal yesterday, didn't you? I'm sorry I wasn't here, but you can't say I didn't warn you that you were looking for trouble."

"You didn't warn me about Mrs. Pearl."

"Christ," he said, "how could I have known she wasn't crippled or whatever? She sure acted as though she was. I don't see how she could have put up with being like that for a whole year when she didn't have to."

"It's hard to understand, isn't it? I guess she lived off her feelings of hatred. They made it worthwhile for her to go through that pretense."

Tom said, "It's scary. If she hadn't come over to kill you, we probably never would have known she faded the other two. Why do you think she went after you?"

"She must have thought I was getting too close to exposing Everett, or maybe 'exposing' isn't the right word. I don't think she believed any of the stuff she considered negative about him; she thought the people who said those things were liars, and it was her duty to stop their lies. More than a duty, really—a need. All that business about Dilly going to be her daughter-in-law and bearing her grandchild, she must have made it up—which isn't to say she didn't believe it. I guess the thing to remember is, never mess with a mother's child. You might end up dead."

He shook his head. "I still can't figure how you knew she was the killer."

"I can't really say I did, although I had become pretty certain that the remaining Six-Packers hadn't done it. If I left them out, I couldn't think of anyone else but her. Remember when you asked me if I thought they'd set fire to my garage and I asked who else it could have been?" I went on to explain how I'd used his theory that people follow a pattern, and the garage fire didn't fit, to figure that it probably had to have been someone else. I said, "I think that's when it really came to me. Etta Pearl was the only other person who might have cared about what was going on. Of course, because of her seeming paralysis I couldn't accept it."

"It's good you stopped her, Rachel. She was a two-time murderer going for three."

"Yes, but I feel sorry for her."

"Are you nuts? She tried to kill you."

"That doesn't change my feeling. She was attempting to protect her child's image."

Tom shook his head. "Women are weird. If men had children, things would be a whole lot different."

"Go home, idiot," I said. Eventually, he did.

The next person to come over was Jordan. He looked pretty grim. "What's the matter?" I said as I let him in.

He didn't answer.

"If you're worried about my involvement with the Dilly Friedman case, don't be. It's over. I caught the murderer yesterday. Incredible as it sounds, it was Etta Pearl." I told him what had happened.

I expected him to act proud of me and to be happy, for me and for him, too. Now he needn't complain that I was mixed up in dangerous affairs. The thing was finished.

"That's good, Rachel," he said in a monotone. "Can we talk?"

I led him to the family room, where Cleome was sitting. When I introduced them, she looked interested but he didn't. He wasn't impolite. It was just that from the way he acted, she didn't have anything to do with him. I didn't like that, but I kept quiet.

"I don't want any," he said when I offered him coffee. "Ah, do you think the little girl could go somewhere else? I really need to talk to you."

Though I sent her out of the room, I could see her lurking in the hall. I didn't mention it to Jordan.

"I've been thinking about us," he said. "I guess I've been thinking about you—and me—since I met you."

That was at his ex-mother-in-law's house, after his ex-wife's funeral. He'd made a good impression on me even then.

"I liked you from the very beginning," he said. "And I never stopped. My kids like you, too. Even Sammy has warmed up to you a little. I know you care about them; I can tell."

I did. In fact, when I first met Jordan, I liked his kids more than I did him. I felt sorry for them and wanted to take care of them. I didn't feel the same need now. It was because of Cleome, I realized. I didn't have the emptiness I'd had before her.

Jordan said, "Maybe that's the worst part of this."

I wasn't following him. "What do you mean?"

"I might as well just say it, Rachel. We don't have a future together."

It wasn't my child being put down; it was me. I said, "Why?"

Cleome stuck her head in the door. "You don't want to marry Miss Rachel?"

I guess he was so ill at ease, it didn't register that she'd been listening. He said, "I'm afraid not."

She stepped further into the room. If there'd been a meter for measuring belligerency, hers would have gone over the top. "What's the matter with you? She—"

It was I who asked her to leave us alone. "Go into the other room," I said. "I really mean it. Jordan and I need to talk."

"But he—"

"It's all right. We didn't want him anyway."

I looked at Jordan. Now he seemed hurt. Good.

I guess my words assured Cleome that I'd survive, so she left with only a little grumbling.

Jordan came over and knelt on the floor beside me, taking my hands into his. I jerked them away. He put his own hands down. "Look, Rachel, it's not that I don't care for you. I do, a lot."

"You have a strange way of showing it."

"I don't have a choice. I can't marry a woman who puts herself in danger of being bludgeoned to death."

"I told you the case was solved. Besides, she was going to use a gun on me."

"That's consoling. What happens if one of these things comes up again?"

"Don't be ridiculous," I said, at the same time wondering if there would be another case. Would there? I liked doing this. It made me feel full of life. And it was such a relief from writing, which was torture to me even though I was obsessed with it.

Jordan looked hesitant. "I . . . don't take this wrong, but I'd like to give your number to someone else. You're too wonderful a person to waste."

If I was so wonderful, how come he was walking away

from me? I didn't say that to him. I also didn't smack him, though I thought about it. I said, "Not interested."

"Just let me tell you about this guy, Rachel. I know you two would like each other. You have a lot in common."

Had he been planning this, planning to fob me off on someone else, to ease his conscience? The situation reminded me of an old movie I'd once taken out called, I think, *The Key*. It starred Sophia Loren and William Holden and was set during World War II, in England. Sophia owned a rooming house that rented to submarine commanders. Before each guy was sent off to sea, most of them to meet a watery death, he'd pass his key, and her, on to the next one. That's how Holden got her, only it was different with him because he loved her. Still, when it was his turn to go to sea, he did the same thing. He was punished for this by drowning in his submarine. I didn't believe there was much chance of this happening to Jordan.

I repeated, "Not interested."

"Change your mind, Rachel. The guy is your type."

"What's his name?" I said, trying to conceal my feelings.

"Hank Rubin."

I frowned. "I don't like it."

Jordan said, "Don't look so down, Rachel. This guy is better."

"Forget it. I'll find my own men."

"I'll send him around."

"I won't open the door."

That's the way we left it. Jordan walked out, and I was alone. Except for Cleome. She came back in the room and said, "What up?"

After I told her, she walked over and hugged me. That was the first time ever. Then we went out for the sundaes. On this occasion, I had a banana split.

After we got home, I lay on the couch, feeling a little sick myself. There was a knock at the door. "Don't answer it," I said.

Cleome went over and peered through the peephole. "Ooh, Miss Rachel," she said, "there's a fine-looking man out there, better looking than that Jordan one. He's holding flowers. I'm going to let him in."

I sat up. "You are not."

She crooned through the door, "Who is it?"

He said, "It's Hank Rubin, Jordan Goldman's friend."

"Come on, Miss Rachel, you got to let him in. At least take a peek at what you're missin'."

I said, "I won't," but then I got off the couch, pushed her out of the way, and looked for myself. She was right. He was definitely fine-looking, tall and lanky, with a long, thin nose that suited his face, dark hair, and dark, intelligent eyes.

I don't know whether he could tell I was staring at him, but in any case, he grinned and held up the flowers. His teeth were perfect.

There's no point being inflexible, I always say. I opened the door and showed him inside. That's how Hank Rubin came into our lives.

If you enjoyed DEADLY HARVEST,
you won't want to miss Ellen Rawlings's first mystery:

THE MURDER LOVER

It wasn't a fitting day for a funeral. It should have been
a bleak afternoon in February, the weather cold and
rainy. Instead, it was early June, the sun was shining, and
the birds were singing their hearts out.

As for me, I should have been in shorts and an old
T-shirt, pedaling my mountain bike through the path-
ways that threaded Fairfield, working up a good sweat.
But I was standing uncomfortably at Har Nebo Cemetery
in a wrinkled blue linen suit and heels. And I didn't even
know the deceased.

We had a lot in common, though, Elspeth Goldman
and I. We both lived in Fairfield, Maryland; we were
both Jewish; and we were both divorced, her once, me
twice. We were even the same age and height, and
people said we resembled each other physically in other
ways as well.

There were differences, too, of course, such as that she
had two children, and I didn't have any. And her life was
over. She'd been murdered several days before, by
person or persons unknown, and I was at her funeral as
one of the mourners.

The site prepared for Elspeth's remains was at the end
of a long row of graves. Most were capped with gray
marble headstones, but not the new ones. Jewish people

don't put up headstones until a year after a funeral. Next June the family would be back for the "unveiling," which is what the showing of the new tombstone is called.

I had said a few words to Paula Cohen, Elspeth's mother, at the funeral home. I didn't know Mrs. Cohen, either. It was Jennie Lavin, Elspeth's grandmother, who was my reason for being there. Although she was forty-five years older than my thirty-five years, she and I were good friends.

Poor Jennie. She'd been really proud of her granddaughter. I wondered how she'd get along after this. She had to be worrying about Elspeth's kids, too.

I noticed that Mrs. Cohen had been joined by two men who looked to be in their late thirties. One was of medium height and stocky, the other, tall and thin. They arranged themselves on either side of her, but not like an honor guard. They looked as though they didn't care for each other much and needed the space between them. I wondered who they were.

I bowed my head as Elspeth's coffin was lowered slowly into the earth. Then the rabbi bent down and whispered into Mrs. Cohen's ear. I saw her shake her head. She'd refused to throw the first clod of dirt on the coffin. Jennie Lavin did it instead.

Other people stepped forward to help fill in a part of the grave, family first. Mrs. Cohen and Mrs. Lavin wept bitterly. Practically everyone was crying by the time this final act, considered a religious privilege, was finished. I felt my own eyes fill with tears. The Jewish religion doesn't make things easy.

Oseh sholom bim'romav hu be'racha'mov, ya'aseh sholom olenu v'al col yisroel v'imru omain.... The ceremony was over. The two men on either side of Mrs. Cohen moved farther away from her, in opposite directions. Now they looked as though they hated each other.

"I hope they don't get into a fistfight here," a voice behind me said.

I turned around quickly, although I knew who it was. The voice was one I heard practically every day.

It belonged to the guy who lived in the town house next to mine. His name was Tom Brant, and he was a detective with the Howard County Police Department. He was a big, growly sort of a guy, with the beginnings of a gut and a heavy beard that caused him to have to shave at least twice a day. He obviously had a high level of testosterone. Perhaps that was what made him such a determined officer; he'd do anything he had to and maybe a little more to solve a case. I knew that about him. We were friends from several years back.

"What are you doing here?" I asked. "I didn't see you before."

He grinned, but the grin faded fast. He must have decided that his expression wasn't appropriate for the occasion. "I was watching through binoculars from an unmarked," he said, his tone as well as his look somber now. "You weren't supposed to see me."

"Okay, I didn't. What were you looking for?"

He shrugged. "Anything."

"And?"

Instead of answering, he took my arm and began walking me down the path that led to the parking lot. I assumed he'd scouted the area previously and recognized my elderly red Toyota.

"And?" I repeated as I hurried to keep up with him. I was a determined person, too.

"Nah, nothing, except that those two guys don't like each other." At my inquiring look, he said, "The short one is her fiancé. He's a banker. The tall one is her ex-husband. He's a mathematician, does some kind of collaborative stuff with scientists at the National Institutes

231

of Health. He and the deceased shared custody of their children."

"Do you think they were jealous? Is that why they looked like they wanted to sock each other?"

"I don't know—yet."

The unspoken promise was there: he would find out.

"Anything you want to tell me?" I asked hopefully.

Again he shrugged. "She was murdered."

"I know that," I said, trying to sound patient and pleasant. "What I'd like to find out is whether it was really an attempted robbery. That's what the papers said."

He shook his head. "I don't know where they got their information. She had seventy-five dollars and a bunch of credit cards spilling out of her handbag. The perp could have scooped them up if that was what he was after. The stuff was lying there on the ground."

I said, "She was killed in her driveway, right?"

"Yeah. Apparently, she'd just parked her car and had gotten out of it when someone grabbed her. The door on the driver's side was still open."

"Too bad she couldn't have gotten back in the car."

"And run over the guy's head! Anyway, there are some pretty high bushes on either side of the driveway, and it looks like he'd been hiding there, waiting for her. My guess is that when he pounced, she dropped her purse."

"Maybe something frightened the killer off after he murdered her," I said.

"I don't think so. This wasn't like a robbery, Rachel. There are some weird things in this case, things that a robber wouldn't do. Take my word for it."

I didn't want to take his word. If there was a story here, I needed to find out about it; the writer in me insisted on it. I do nonfiction articles for a living, some of them investigative, and I know how to dig and not give up. "Oh, really?" I said. "Like what?"

"I'm not supposed to talk about it."

"Was she molested?" I asked.

"Nah."

"Then what?"

"Well, the way she died was weird. But that's part of what I can't talk about, so stop asking me, Rachel. Okay?"

I couldn't stop. "If you say so," I murmured, then asked, "But wasn't she strangled? That's what I read."

I guess he couldn't stop, either. "Yeah, she was strangled. But it wasn't an ordinary strangling."

I took a guess that she had been strangled with something other than someone's hands. "Oh, come on. You can trust me. I won't tell Nancy. Besides, she already let me know there was a murder weapon."

Nancy Martin was one of my closest friends. She ran the bimonthly magazine *The Howard County Target*; I'd written quite a few articles for it. She often was privy to things that weren't public knowledge. Actually, Nancy had said she didn't know if there'd been a murder weapon.

"You mean someone told her about the stocking? I'd like to find out who the hell it was."

My ruse had worked. I felt kind of ashamed, but pleased, too. "Nancy didn't mention a stocking," I confessed. "I'm afraid I tricked you, but now that I know, you might as well tell me the rest, don't you think?"

"Damn it, Rachel, that's not funny. This is murder, not a game. A woman who had two kids and was going to be married is dead."

It was my turn to be embarrassed. "I'm sorry. All I can say in my defense is that I can't help being curious and I

233

wasn't lying when I said I wouldn't tell Nancy. I won't tell anybody. That's a promise."

He shrugged, a gesture that was habitual with him. "Okay, I believe you. The truth is, she was strangled with half a stocking. We didn't tell that to the reporters, though. You wouldn't believe how many nuts would come forward and confess to killing her just that way if we did. We have to be sure we get the right guy."

I frowned at him. "I don't know what you mean by 'half' of a stocking."

"I mean some guy took a pair of—what do you call them?—panty hose and cut them down the middle. He used one of them to strangle her."

"I agree with you: That's weird. Why would he use just one?"

"I don't know. Maybe he's saving the other half for someone else."

Did he expect me to laugh? In a way, I hoped so, because that would mean he didn't believe it himself and was just joking. I wanted him to be joking. Just in case, though, I didn't laugh.

THE MURDER LOVER
by Ellen Rawlings

Published by Fawcett Books.
Available in your local bookstore.